"Beyond," asked the Visitor. "Farther than Old Watcher. What's there?"

"The Outlands," said Fauconred. "Swamps, marshes, desolation."

"And beyond that?"

"Beyond that? Nothing."

"How, nothing?"

Fauconred peered into a tiny goatskin-bound book, licking a thick thumb to turn its fine pages. He found his place and turned the book into the light to read. The Visitor bent close to him to hear over the wind and the hooves. Carefully Fauconred made out the words:

"The world is founded on a pillar which is founded on the Deep.

"Of the world, it is a great circle; its center is the lake island called the Hub and its margins are waste and desolate.

"Of the pillar, it is of adamant. Its width is nearly the width of the world, and now man knows its length for it is founded on the Deep. The pillar supports the world like the arm and hand of an infinite Servant, holding a platter up..."

The Deep by John Crowley
author of *Little, Big*, *Engine Summer* and *Beasts*

Other Bantam Books by John Crowley
Ask your bookseller for the books you may have missed.

BEASTS
ENGINE SUMMER
LITTLE BIG

THE DEEP

John Crowley

BANTAM BOOKS
TORONTO · NEW YORK · LONDON · SYDNEY

THE DEEP

**A Bantam Book / published by arrangement with
Doubleday & Company, Inc.**

PRINTING HISTORY
Doubleday edition published April 1975
Bantam edition / January 1984

ISBN 0-553-23944-9

Published simultaneously in the United States and Canada

PRINTED IN THE UNITED STATES OF AMERICA

O   0 9 8 7 6 5 4 3 2 1

In memoriam
J.B.C.

PRINCIPAL CHARACTERS

The Blacks:
> King Little Black
> The Queen, his wife
> Black Harrah, the Queen's lover
> Young Harrah, his son
> A bastard son of Farin the Black

The Reds:
> Red Senlin
> Red Senlin's Son (later King)
> Sennred, Red Senlin's younger son
> Redhand
> Old Redhand, his father
> Younger Redhand, his brother
> Caredd, his wife
> Mother Caredd
> Fauconred

The Just:
> Nyamé, whose name is called Nod
> The Neither-nor
> Adar

The Grays:
> Mariadn, the Arbiter
> Learned Redhand, Redhand's brother and later
>   Arbiter

Endwives, Ser and Norin

And a nameless one from Elsewhere called variously
> Visitor
> Secretary
> Recorder

Canst thou draw out Leviathan with an hook?
Or his tongue with a cord which thou lettest down?
Will he make a covenant with thee?
And wilt thou take him for a servant for ever?
Lay thine hand upon him,
Remember the battle, do no more.

Job

THE DEEP

ONE

.

VISITOR

1

After the skirmish, two Endwives found him lying in the darkness next to the great silver egg. It took them only a moment to discover that he was neither male nor female; somewhat longer to decide whether he was alive or dead. Alive, said one; the other wasn't sure for how long; anyway, they took him up on their rude stretcher and walked with him nearly a mile to where a station of theirs had been set up a week before when the fighting had started; there they laid him out.

They had thought to patch him up however they could in the usual way, but when they began working they found that he was missing more than sex. Parts of him seemed made of something other than flesh, and from the wound at the back of his head the blood that flowed seemed viscous, like oil. When the older of the two caught a bit of it on a glass, and held it close to the lamplight, she gasped: it was alive—it flowed in tiny swirls ever, like oil in alcohol, but finer, blue within crimson. She showed her sister. They sat down then, unsure, looking at the figure on the pallet; ghastly pale he was in the lamplight and all hairless. They weren't afraid; they had seen too much horror to fear anything. But they were unsure.

All night they watched him by lamplight. Toward dawn he began to move slightly, make sounds. Then spasms, violent, though he seemed in no pain—it was as though puppet strings pulled him. They cushioned his white damaged head; one held his thrashing arms while the other prepared a calming drug. When she had it ready, though, they paused, looking at each other, not knowing what effect this most trusted of all their secrets might have. Finally, one shrugging and the other with lips pursed, they forced some between his tightclosed teeth.

Well, he was a man to this extent; in minutes he lay quiet, breathing regularly. They inspected, gingerly and almost with repulsion, the wound in his head; it had already begun to pucker closed, and bled no more. They decided there was little they could do but wait. They stood over him a moment; then the older signaled, and they stepped out of the sod hut that was their station into the growing dawn.

The great gray heath they walked on was called the Drumskin. Their footsteps made no sound on it, but when the herds of horses pastured there rode hard, the air filled with a long hum like some distant thunder, a hum that could be heard Inward all the way to the gentle folded farmland called the Downs, all the way Outward to the bleak stone piles along the Drumsedge, outposts like Old Watcher that they could see when the road reached the top of a rise, a dim scar on the flat horizon far away.

They heard, dimly, that thunder as they stood at the top of the rise, their brown skirts plucked at by wind. They looked down into the gray grass bottom that last night's struggle had covered, a wide depression in the Drumskin that everywhere was pocketed with such hiding-places. This pocket held now four dead men or women; the burying spades of the Endwives, left last night; and an egg made of some dull silver, as high as a man, seemingly solid.

"What," said the younger then, "if no one knows of him but us?"

"We must tell his comrades, whichever they be, that we have him. It's the Way. We must tell the comrades of any survivor that he lives. And only his comrades."

"And how are we to know which—if either—were his comrades? I don't think either were."

The old one thought.

"Maybe," said the younger, "we should tell both."

"One side would probably gain an advantage, and the other probably not. The Protector Redhand might arrest him, and the Just be disadvantaged. The Just might kill him, and the Protector be disadvantaged. Worse: there might be a battle waged over him, that we would be the cause of."

"Well . . ."

"It's happened. That Endwives not taking care which side might be advantaged have caused death. It's happened. To our shame."

The other was silent. She looked up to where the Morning Star shone steadily. The home of the borning, as the Evening Star was of the dead.

"Perhaps he won't last the day," she said.

They called him Visitor. His strange wound healed quickly, but the two sisters decided that his brain must have been damaged. He spoke rarely, and when he did, in strange nonsense syllables. He listened carefully to everything said to him, but understood nothing. He seemed neither surprised nor impatient nor grateful about his circumstances; he ate when he was given food and slept when they slept.

The week had been quiet. After the battle into which the Visitor had intruded, the Just returned to the Nowhere they could disappear to, and the Protector's men returned to the farms and the horse-gatherings, to

other battles in the Protector's name. None had passed
for several days except peatcutters from the Downs.

Toward the close of a clear, cold day, the elder
Endwife, Ser, made her slow circular way home across
the Drumskin. In her wide basket were ten or so boxes
and jars, and ever she knelt where her roving eye saw
in the tangle of gray grass an herb or sprout of something useful. She'd pluck it, crush and sniff it, choose
with pursed lips a jar for it. When it had grown too dark
to see them any more, she was near home; yellow
lamplight poured from the open door. She straightened
her stiff back and saw the stars and planets already
ashine; whispered a prayer and covered her jars from
the Evening Star, just in case.

When she stepped through the door, she stopped
there in the midst of a "Well..." Fell silent, pulled the
door shut and crept to a chair.

The Visitor was talking.

The younger Endwife, Norin, sat rapt before him,
didn't turn when her sister entered. The Visitor, motionless on the bed, drew out words with effort, as
though he must choose each one. But he was talking.

"I remember," he was saying, "the sky. That—egg,
you call it. I was placed. In it. And. Separated. From
my home. Then, descending. In the egg. To here."

"Your home," said Norin. "That star."

"You say a star," the Visitor said blankly. "I think, it
can't have been a star. I don't know how, I know it, but,
I do."

"But it circled the world. In the evening it rose from
the Deep. And went overhead. In the morning it
passed again into the Deep."

"Yes."

"For how long?"

"I don't know. I was made there."

"There were others there. Your parents."

"No. Only me. It was a place not much larger than
the egg."

He sat expressionless on the edge of the bed, his long pale hands on his knees. He looked like a statue. Norin turned to her sister, her eyes shining.

"Is he mad now?" said Ser. Her sister's face darkened.

"I . . . don't know. Only, just today he learned to speak. This morning when you left he began. He learned 'cup' and 'drink,' like a baby, and now see! In one day, he's speaking so! He learned so fast . . ."

"Or remembered," Ser said, arising slowly with her eyes on the Visitor. She bent over him and looked at his white face; his eyes were black holes. She intended to be stern, to shock him; it sometimes worked. Her hand moved to the shade of the lamp, turned it so the lamplight fell full on him.

"You were born inside a star in the sky?" she asked sharply.

"I wasn't born," said the Visitor evenly. "I was made."

Ser's old hand shook on the lampshade, for the lamplight fell on eyes that had neither iris nor pupil, but were a soft, blank violet, infinitely deep and without reflection.

"How . . . Who are you?"

The Visitor opened his thin lips to speak, but was silent. Ser lowered the lampshade.

Then Ser sat down beside her sister, and they listened to the Visitor attempt to understand himself out loud to them, here and there helping with a guessed word or fact.

"When the egg opened," said the Visitor, "and I came out into the darkness, I knew. I can remember knowing. Who I am, what had made me, for what purpose. I came out . . . bearing all this, like . . . like a . . ."—pointing to Ser's basket.

"A gift," said Norin.

"A bundle," said Ser.

"But then, almost as soon as I arose, there were men, above me, dark, silent; I don't think they saw me; something long and thin strapped to each back . . ."

"Yes," said Norin. "The Just."

"And before I could speak to them, others came, with, with..."

"Horses," said Ser. "Yes. Protector Redhand's men."

"I ran up the—the bank, just as these two collided. There were cries, I cried out, to make them see me. There was a noise that filled up the air."

"A Gun," said Norin.

The Visitor fell silent then. The Endwives waited. The lamp buzzed quietly.

"The next thing I remember," he said at last, "is that cup, and drinking from it today."

Ser pondered, troubled. She would still prefer to think him mad; but the blank eyes, now velvet black, the viscous, living blood, the sexlessness... perhaps it was she who was mad. "How," she began, "did you learn to speak so well, so fast?"

He shook his head slowly. "It seems... easy, I don't know... It must be—part of what I was made to do. Yes. It is. I was made so, so that I could speak to you."

"'You,'" said Ser doubtfully. "And who is 'you'?"

"You," said the Visitor. "All of you."

"There is no all of us," Norin said. "There are the Folk, but they aren't all of us. Because there are also the Just, with their Guns..."

"Warriors for the Folk," said Ser. "So they claim. They make war on the Protectors, who own the land, to take it from them and return it to the Folk. Secret war, assassination. They are known only to each other. And yet most Folk stand aside from the Just; and in hundreds of years of this nothing has changed, not truly. But the war goes on. You tried to speak to both of them, Just and the Protector's men, together; so you see."

"Even the Protectors," Norin said. "They own the land, they are the chief men..."

"They, then," said the Visitor.

"But they are divided into factions, intrigues, alliances. As bitter toward each other as they are toward the Just."

"The Reds and the Blacks," said Norin.

"Old quarrels." Ser sighed. "We Endwives come after battles, not before them. We help the hurt to live, and bury the dead."

"More often bury than help," said her sister.

"We are pledged neither to aid nor hurt in any quarrel. And . . . I suppose it can't be explained to you, but . . . the world is so divided that if anyone knew of you but us, you would be used for a counter in their game. And the death that came in the next moves— if death came—would be on our hands."

From his smooth face they couldn't tell if he had grasped any of this. "The Folk," he said at last.

Ser pursed her lips. He wouldn't leave it. "They aren't much used to being spoken to," she said drily. "Except by the Grays."

"Grays?"

"A brotherhood; lawyers and scholars; arbiters, priests, keepers of wisdom . . ." He had turned to her. "And what," she asked softly, "will you tell them then?"

She saw, not by any change in his face, but by the flexing of his long fingers, that he was in some torment of ignorance.

"I don't remember," he said at last.

"Well."

His pale hands ceased working and lay quiet on his sharp knees. His face grew, if possible, still more remote; he looked ahead at nothing, as though waiting for some internal advice. Then he said, with neither patience nor hope: "Perhaps, if I wait, something will return to me. Some direction, some other part of the way I am made, that will let me know the next thing to do."

Somewhere far off there grew a soft hum, indeterminate, coming from nowhere, growing louder that way, then louder this way. Riders on the Drumskin; the heath was speaking. Ser rose heavily, her eyes on the door, and moved to turn down the lamp.

"Perhaps it will," she said. "Until it does, you will stay here. Inside. And be silent."

The drumbeat grew steadily more distinct; the universal hum resolved itself into individual horses riding hard. Then cries, just outside. And Ser couldn't bar the door, because an Endwife's door is never barred.

Then there stood in the doorway a thick barrel of a man, bull-necked, shorn of all but a fuzz of steely hair. Dressed in leather, all colored red. Behind him two others in red carried between them a third, head bent back, open mouth moaning, red jacket brighter red with blood.

The barrel-man began to speak, but stopped when he saw someone sitting on the bed, pale and unmoving, regarding him with dark, calm eyes.

The Defender Fauconred disliked pens. He disliked paper and ink. On stormy days (which were growing more frequent as the year turned) or in the evenings after the horsegathering, he liked to stretch out on the pallet in his tent with a mug of blem-and-warm-water and stare at the pictures the living charcoal made in the brazier.

But once a week, every week, he must push his barrel shape into a camp chair and trim the lamp; sharpen two or three pens; lay out paper and mix ink; sit, sighing, humming, running thick fingers over his stubble of steel-gray hair; and finally begin.

"The Defender Fauconred to the Great Protector Redhand, greetings etc." That part was easy.

"We are this day within sight of Old Watcher, on a line between it and the Little Lake, as far from the lake as you can see a white horse on a clear day." He stopped, dipped his pen. "The herd numbers now one hundred five. Of these, forty-seven are stallions. Of the yearlings, the Protector will remember there were forty-nine in the spring. We have found thirty. Of all the horses, one is crippled, two have the bloat, and we have found three dead, one the old painted stallion the Protector mentioned.

"The Horse-master says the herd should number in all one hundred forty, counting in all dead & wounded & sick. He says the rains will be heavy in a week or two weeks. I think one. Unless other word comes from the Protector, we will be herding homeward in about ten days and reach the Downs before Barnolsweek. I will then come to the Hub with the Guard, bringing such horses as the Horse-master chooses, to the number twenty or as convenient."

Chewing on the end of the pen, Fauconred assembled the other news in his head, sighed, bent again over the paper.

"Also, the roan mare with the white eye the Protector mentioned has been found, and is in health.

"Also, we discovered one lying in ambush, with a Gun. When we questioned him he answered nothing, but looked always proud. He is hanged, and his Gun broken.

"Also, a man of my guard has been shot with a Gun, and though he will live, we are more alert.

"Also . . ."

Also. The Defender put down his splayed pen and looked to where the Visitor stood outside the tent, unmoving, patient, a dark shape in the brown Endwife's cloak against the growing thunderclouds.

Also. How could he be explained to the Protector? Fauconred drew out a fresh sheet, picked up a new pen. "Protector, I have found one sheltered by the Endwives, one neither male nor female, having no hair, who says he is not of the world but was made in the sky." He read it over, biting his lip. "I swear on my oaths to you and ours that it is true." The harder he swore, the more fantastical it sounded. "Perhaps," he began, and struck it out. It was not his place to perhaps about it. "He asks permission to come to the Protector. I know nothing to do but bring him to you." *Defender*, the old Endwife had said to him, *I charge you as you shall ever need me or mine, let no harm come to him.* He moved the pen above the paper in an agony of doubt. "I have promised him my protection. I hope . . ." Struck out. "I know the Protector will honor my promise." And he signed it: "The Drumskin, Bannsweek, by my hand, the Defender Fauconred, your servant."

He folded the letters separately, the ordinary and the preposterous, took wax, lit it in the lamp, and with his chin in his hand let the wax clot in bright crimson drops like blood on the fold of each. He pressed his ring, which showed a hand lifting a cup, into the glittering clots and watched them dry hard and perfect. He shook his head, and with a grunt pulled himself from his chair.

The Visitor still stood motionless, looking out over the gray evening heath. The wind had increased, and plucked at the brown cloak that the younger Endwife had wrapped him in; that was his disguise, for now, and Fauconred felt his sexlessness strongly seeing him in it.

"The herdsmen have returned," the Visitor said.

"Yes," said Fauconred.

They sat their ponies gracefully, wrapped to their eyes in dark windings that fluttered around them like bannerets. They moved the quick herd before them with flicks of long slim lashes and cries that, wind-borne, came up strangely enlarged to where Fauconred and the Visitor stood. Beyond, Old Watcher was lost in thick storm clouds that were moving over fast. The storm was the color of new iron, and trailed a skirt of rain; it was lit within by dull yellow lightnings. The roans and whites and painteds thundered before it, eyes panicky; the Drumskin's thunder as they ran was answered by the storm's drums, mocked by the chuckle of Fauconred's tent-cloths rippling.

"Beyond," said the Visitor, lifting his gentle voice

against the noise. "Farther than Old Watcher. What's there?"

"The Outlands," said Fauconred. "Swamps, marshes, desolation."

"And beyond that?"

"Beyond that? Nothing."

"How, nothing?"

"The world has to end eventually," said Fauconred. "And so it does. They say there's an edge, a lip. As on a tray, you know. And then nothing."

"There can't be nothing," said the Visitor simply.

"Well, it's not the world," said Fauconred. He held out a lined palm. "The world is like this. Beyond the world is like beyond my hand. Nothing."

The Visitor shook his head. Fauconred, with an impatient sigh, waved and shouted to a knot of red-jacketed horsemen below. One detached himself from the group and started up the long rise. Fauconred turned and ducked back inside his tent.

He returned with the two letters under his arm, peering into a tiny goatskin-bound book, licking a thick thumb to turn its fine figured pages. He found his place, and turned the book into the light to read. The Visitor bent close to him to hear over the wind and the hooves. Carefully Fauconred made out words:

"The world is founded on a pillar which is founded on the Deep.

"Of the world, it is a great circle; its center is the lake island called the Hub and its margins are waste and desolate.

"Of the pillar, it is of adamant. Its width is nearly the width of the world, and no man knows its length for it is founded on the Deep. The pillar supports the world like the arm and hand of an infinite Servant holding a platter up."

He turned the page and with a finger held down its snapping corner. "The sky is the Deep above," he went on, "and as the Deep is heavy, so the sky is light. Each day the sun rises from the Deep, passes overhead, and falls again within the Deep; each night it passes under the Deep and hastens to the place where it arose. Between the world and the sun travel seven Wanderers, which likewise arise and descend into the Deep, but with an irregular motion . . ."

He closed the book. Up the rise came the red-jacketed man he had summoned. The rider pulled up, his horse snorted, and Fauconred took the bridle.

"It's possible," said the Visitor.

"Possible?" Fauconred shouted. "Possible?" He handed up the two letters to the beardless redjacket. "To the Protector Redhand, at his father's house, in the City."

The wind had begun to scream. "Tell the Protector," Fauconred shouted over the wind's voice. The boy leaned down to him. "Tell the Protector I bring him a . . . a visitor."

2

There are seven windows in the Queen's bedroom in the Citadel that is the center of the City that is on the lake island called the Hub in the middle of the world.

Two of the seven windows face the tower stones and are dark; two overlook inner courtyards; two face the complex lanes that wind between the high, blank-faced mansions of the Protectorate; and the seventh, facing the steep Street of Birdsellers and, beyond, a crack in the ring of mountains across the lake, is always filled at night with stars. When wind speaks in the mountains, it whispers in this window, and makes the fine brown bed hangings dance.

Because the Queen likes light to make love by, there is a tiny lamp lit within the bed hangings. Black Harrah, the Queen's lover of old, dislikes the light; it makes him think as much of discovery as of love. But then, one is not the Queen's lover solely at one's own pleasure.

If there were now a discoverer near, say on the balcony over the double door, or in the curtained corridor that leads to the servants' stairs, he would see the great bed, lit darkly from within. He would see the great, thick body of the Queen struggling impatiently against Black Harrah's old lean one, and hear their cries rise and subside. He might, well-hidden, stay to watch them cease, separate, lie somnolent; might hear shameful things spoken; and later, if he has waited, hear them consider their realm's affairs, these two, the Queen and her man, the Great Protector Black Harrah.

"No, no," Black Harrah answers to some question.

"I fear," says the Queen.

"There are ascendancies," says Black Harrah sleepily. "Binding rules, oaths sworn. Fixed as stars."

"New stars are born. The Grays have found one."

"Please. One thing at a time."

"I fear Red Senlin."

"He is no new star. If ever a man were bound by oaths . . ."

"He hates me."

"Yes," Harrah says.

"He would be King."

"No."

"If he . . ."

"I will kill him."

"If he kills you . . . ?"

"My son will kill him. If his sons kill my son, my son's sons will kill his. Enough?"

Silence. The watcher (for indeed he is there, on the balcony over the half-open double door, huddled into a black, watching pile, motionless) nods his head in tiny approving nods, well pleased.

The Queen starts up, clutching the bedclothes around her.

"What is it?" Black Harrah asks.

"A noise."

"Where?"

"There. On the stair. Footsteps."

"No."

"Yes!"

Feet grow loud without. Shouts of the Queen's guards, commands, clash of arms. Feet run. Suddenly, swinging like a monkey from the balcony, grasping handholds and dropping to the floor, the watcher, a tiny man all in black. Crying shrilly, he forces the great door shut and casts the bolt just as armed red-coated men approach without. The clash of the bolt is still echoing when armed fists pound from the other side:

"Open! In the name of the Great Protector Red Senlin!"

The watcher now clings to the bolt as though his little arms could aid it and screams: "Leave! Go away! I order you!"

"We seek the traitor Black Harrah, for imprisonment in the King's name..."

"Fool! Go! It is I who command you, I, your King, and as you truly owe me, leave!"

The noise without ceases for a moment. The King Little Black turns to the bed. Black Harrah is gone. The King's wife stands upright on the bed, huge and naked.

"Fly!" the King shouts. She stands unmoving, staring; then with a boom the door is hammered on with breaking tools. The Queen turns, takes up a cloak, and runs away down the servants' corridor, her screaming maidservants after her. The door behind the King begins to crack.

Because the island City lies within a great deep cup, whose sides are mountains, dawn comes late there and evening early. And even when the high spires of the

Citadel, which is at the top of the high-piled City, are touched with light filtering through the blue-green forests, and then the High City around it and then the old-fashioned mansions mostly shuttered are touched, and then the old inns and markets, and the narrow streets of the craftsmen, and then the winding water-stairs, piles, piers, ramparts, esplanades and wharfs—even then the still lake, which has no name, is black. Mist rises from its depths like chill breath, obscuring the flat surface so that it seems no lake but a hole pierced through the fabric of the world, and the shadowy, broad-nosed craft that ride its margins—and the City itself—seem suspended above the Deep.

But when the first light does strike the Citadel, the whole world knows it's high morning; and though the watermen can still see only stars, they are about their business. The Protectorate has ever feared a great bridge over the lake that couldn't be cut down at need, and so the four bridges that hang like swaying ribbons from the High City gates are useless for anything but walkers or single riders. The watermen's business is therefore large, and necessary; they are a close clan, paid like servants yet not servants, owing none, singing their endless, tuneless songs, exchanging their jokes that no one else laughs at.

It was the watermen in their oiled goatskins who first saw that Red Senlin had returned from the Outlands, because it was they who carried him and his armed riders and his fierce Outland captains into the City. The watermen didn't care if Red Senlin wanted to be King; it's well-known that the watermen, "neither Folk nor not," care only for the fee.

Fauconred had put the Visitor on early watch, to make some use of him; but when the first chill beams silvered the Drum fog he woke, shivered with premonition, and went to find the Visitor.

He was still watching. Impervious apparently to loneliness, weariness, cold, he still looked out over the quadrant assigned to him.

"Quit now," Fauconred said to him hoarsely, taking his elbow. "Your watch is long over." The man (if man he was) turned from his watch and went with Fauconred, without question or complaint.

"But—what," he asked when they sat by Fauconred's fire, "was I to watch for?"

"Well, the Just," Fauconred said. "They can be anywhere." He leaned toward the Visitor, as though he might even here be overheard, and the Visitor bent close to hear. "They draw lots by some means, among themselves. So I hear. And each of them then has a Protector, or Defender, that he is pledged to murder. Secretly, if possible. And so you see, since it's by lots, and nothing personal, you'll never know the man. You can come face to face with him; he seems a cottager or . . . or anyone. You talk. The place is lonely. Suddenly, there is the Gun."

The Visitor considered this, touching the place on his head where he had been hurt. "Then how could I watch for one?" he asked.

Fauconred, confused, tossed sticks angrily into the fire, but made no other answer. Day brightened. Ahead lay the Downs at last . . .

It was a waterside inn.

"Secretly," the cloaked man said. "And quickly."

"You are . . ."

"A . . . merchant. Yes. What does it matter?" His old, lean hand drew a bag from within a shapeless, hooded traveler's cloak. It made a solid sound on the inn table.

The girl he spoke to was a waterman's daughter. Her long neck was bare; her blond, almost white hair cut off short like a boy's. She turned, looked out a tiny window that pierced the gray slatting of the inn wall. Above the

mountains the sky had grown pale; below, far below, the
lake was dark.

"The bridges?" she asked.

"Closed. Red Senlin has returned."

"Yes."

"His mob has closed the bridges."

"Then it must be illegal to ferry."

The other, after a moment, added a second bag to the
table. The girl regarded neither. "Get me," the traveler
said, "three days' food. A sword. And get your father to
take me to the mountain road before daybreak. I'll
double that."

The girl sat staring a moment, and then rose quickly,
picking up the two bags. "I'll take you," she said, and
turned away into the darkness of the inn. The traveler
watched her go; then sat turning this way and that,
looking ever out the tiny window at the pre-dawn sky.
Around him a dark crowd of watermen sat; he heard
bits of muttered conversation.

"There were oaths sworn."

Someone spat disgustedly.

"He's rightful King."

"Yes. Much as any."

"Black Harrah will hang him."

"Or maybe just hang."

Laughter. Then: "Where is Redhand?"

"Redhand. Redhand knows."

"Yes. Much as any."

Suddenly the girl was before him. Her long neck rose
columnlike out of a thick cloak she had wrapped over
her oiled goatskins—and over a bundle which she held
before her.

"The sword?" he whispered.

"Come," she said.

There was a dank, endless stairway within the warren
of the inn that gave out finally onto an esplanade still
hooded in dark and fog. He followed her close, starting
at noises and shapes.

"The sword," he whispered at her ghostly back.
"Now."

"Here, the water-stairs. Down."

She turned sharply around the vast foot of pillar that
supported waterfront lodges above, and started down
the ringing stone stairway faster than he could follow. In
a moment she was gone; he stumbled quickly after her,
alone now, as though there were no other thing in the
world than this descent, no other guide but the sound
of her footsteps ahead.

Then her footsteps ceased. He stopped. There was a
lapping of water somewhere.

"Stop," he said.

"I have," she answered.

"Where?"

"Here."

The last step gave out on a gravelly bit of shingle,
barely walking space. He could see nothing ahead at
first; took three timid steps and saw her, a tall blank
ghost, indistinct, just ahead.

"Oh. There."

"Yes."

He crept forward. Her figure grew clearer: the paleness
of her white head, the dark cloak, in her hand the . . .

In her hand the Gun.

"Black Harrah," she said.

"No," he said.

"Justice," she said.

The Gun she held in both hands was half as long as
an arm, and its great bore was like a mouth; it clicked
when she fired it, hissed white smoke, and exploded
like all rage and hatred. The stone ball shattered Black
Harrah; without a cry he fell, thrown against the stairs,
wrapped in a shower of his own blood.

High above, on the opposite side of the City, by the
gate called Goforth from which a long tongue of bridge
came out, a young man commanded other men for the

first time; a dark, small man destined by birth so to command; who felt sure now, as dawn began to silhouette the mountains against the sky, that he was in fact fitted for the work, and whose hand began to ease at last his nervous grip on his sword handle. He sighed deeply. There would be no Black reprisals. His men began to slouch against the ancient bridge pilings. One laughed. Day had come, and they were all alive.

The young man's name was Sennred; he was the younger of the two sons of Red Senlin, he who had come out of exile in the Outlands to reclaim his rightful place at the King's side by whatever means necessary.

That the Great Protector Red Senlin had been unjustly kept away from King Little Black's side by Black Harrah; that he came now to help the King throw off Black Harrah's tyranny; that his whole desire was to cleanse odiousness and scandal from the Citadel (and if that meant Black Harrah's arrest, so be it)—all this the young Sennred had by heart and would have argued fiercely to any who suspected his father's motives; but at the same time, as many can who are young and quick and loyal, Sennred could hold a very different view of things . . .

A century almost to the day before this pregnant dawn, a crime had torn the ancient and closely woven fabric of this world: a Great Protector, half-brother of King Ban, had seized from King Ban's heir the iron crown. King Ban's heir was the son of King Red. The Great Protector's name was Black. To the family Red and all its branches, allies, dependents, it mattered nothing that King Red's son was a foul cripple, a tyrannous boy in love with blood; he was Ban's heir. To the family Black and its equally extensive connections what mattered was that the crown had fitted Black's head, that the great legal fraternity, the Grays, had confirmed him, and his son, and his son's son. There had been uprisings, rebellions; lately there had been a brief battle at Senlinsdown, and King Little Black, childless, had accepted Red Senlin as his heir. So there had been no war—not quite; only, the world had divided itself further into factions, the factions had eaten up the unaligned, had grown paid armies each to protect itself from the other; the factions now waited, poised.

Red Senlin was King Red's true heir. He had learned that as a boy. He had never for a moment forgotten it.

And his younger son Sennred knew in his heart who was truly the King, and why Red Senlin had come back from the Outlands.

Around him, above him, the great City houses of the Protectorate had begun to awaken, such as were used; many were empty. There was, he knew, one sleeping army in the City large enough to decide, before noon, whether or not the world would change today; it was housed in and around that dark pile where now lamplight glimmered in tiny windows—the Harbor, the house of the family Redhand.

The Redhands would be waking to a new world, Sennred thought; and his hand tightened again on his sword handle.

At the head table in the great hall smoky with torches and loud with the noise of half a hundred Redhand dependents breaking their fast, Old Redhand sat with his three sons.

There was Redhand, the eldest, his big warrior's hands tearing bread he didn't eat, a black beard around his mouth.

There was the Gray brother, Learned, beside him. The gray that Learned Redhand wore was dark, darker than the robes of Grays far older than himself, dark and convoluted as a thundercloud, and not lightened by a bit of red ribbon pinned within its folds.

There was, lastly, Younger. Younger was huddled down in his chair, turning an empty cup, looking as though someone had struck him and he didn't know how to repay it.

When the red-jacketed messenger approached them they all looked up, expectantly; but it was only letters from the Drum, from Fauconred; Redhand tucked them away unread . . . "The Queen," he said to Learned, "has fled, Outward. No one knows how she escaped, or where Black Harrah is."

"Red Senlin let them slip."

"He would. Graceless as a dog among birds." Redhand's voice was a deep, gritty growl, a flaw left by the same sword that had drawn a purple line up his throat to his ear; he wore the beard to hide it.

"Where is Young Harrah?" Learned asked. The friendship between Black Harrah's son and Red Senlin's was well-known; they did little to hide it, though their fathers raged at it.

"Not imprisoned. At Red Senlin's Son's request—or demand. He will fly too; he must live. Join his father . . ."

"Will Red Senlin be King now?" Younger asked. "Does he wish it?"

"He could bring war with his wishing," Learned said. "He would."

"Perhaps," Redhand said, "he can be dissuaded."

"We can try," Learned said. "The reasons . . ."

Trembling with suppressed rage, his father cut across him. "You talk as though he were a naughty child. He is your uncle, and twice your age."

"He must listen, anyway," said Younger. "Because he can't do it without us. He knows that."

"*Must listen*," Old Redhand said bitterly. "He will abide by your wishes." His hands were tight fists on the table.

"He will," Redhand said.

"And if he won't," Old Redhand shouted, rising out of his seat, "what then? Will you cut off his head?"

"Stop," Learned said. "The guests . . ."

"He is here because of you," Old Redhand shouted at his eldest son. "You, the Great Protector Redhand. Because of you and your army he thinks he can do this thing."

"He is rightful King," said Younger softly, drawing in spilled drink on the table.

"Little Black is King," said his brother Redhand.

"*My* King," said his father, "shortly to be murdered, no doubt, whom I fought for in the Outlands, and against the Just, and whom Red Senlin fought for and in the old days . . ."

"The old days," came his eldest's gritty voice, cold with disgust. "If time turned around, you could all be young again. But against the advice of the old, it keeps its course." He rose, took up his gloves. "And maybe it means to see Red Senlin King. If by my strength, then by my strength. You are gone foolish if you stand in our way."

His father rose too, and was about to speak, shout, curse; Redhand stood hard, ready to receive: and then there was a noise at the back of the hall; messengers, belted and armed, were making their way to the head table. Their news, rippling through the assembly as though from a cast stone, reached the head table before its bearers:

The Great Protector Black Harrah is dead. The richest man in the world, the Queen's lover, the King's King, has been shot with a Gun on the margin of the un-plumbed lake.

The way from Redhand's house to the Citadel lay along the Street of Birdsellers, up the steep way through the Gem Market, along Bellmaker's Street; throngs of City people, lashed by rumor, called out to Redhand, and he waved but made no replies; his brother Younger and a crowd of his redjackets made a way for them through the frightened populace. "Redhand!" they called to him. "Redhand . . . !"

They said of the family Redhand that they had not walked far from the cottage door, which in an age-long scheme of things was true. Old Redhand's great-grandfather was the first Defender; he had been born merely a tenant of a Red lord whose line was extinguished by war and the assassinations of the Just. But it had always been so; there was no Protector, however great, who somewhere within the creases of history had not a farmer or a soldier or even a thief tucked.

Why one would wish to plot and strive to rise from the quiet pool of the Folk to be skimmed from the top by war, feud, and assassination was a question all the poets asked and none answered. The Protectorate was a selfish martyrdom, it had never a place empty. The laws and records of inheritance filled musty floors of the Citadel. Inheritance was the chief business of all courts of the Grays. Inheritance was the slow turning of this still world, and the charting of its ascendancies and declinations took up far more of the world's paper and ink than the erratic motions of its seven moons.

At Kingsgate, men Redhand recognized as old soldiers of Red Senlin's, wearing ill-fitting King's-men's coats, barred their passage. Redhand summoned an unshaven one with a pot in his hand. When the man came close, frankly comradely, but shaking his head, Redhand leaned over and took his collar in a strangling grip.

"Goat," he growled, "get your mummers out of my way or I'll ride them down."

He would almost have preferred them not to move.

Their hooves clattered down Kingsgate Alley between the walls of blank-faced, doorless mansions, pierced only far above by round windows. Somewhere above them a shutter clashed shut, echoing off the cool, shadowed stone walls.

Down at the puddly end of the alley was a tiny doorway called Defensible, a jackhole merely in the great curving wall of a rotunda: one of only three ways into the vastness of the Citadel.

The rotunda that Defensible let them into one by one was unimaginably old, crudely but grandly balconied, balustraded, arched and pierced. They said that this rotunda must be all that the Citadel was, once; that it was built up on older, smaller places that had left traces in its walls and doors. They said that the center of its figured stone floor was the exact center of the world; they said that the thousand interlaced pictures that covered the floor, once they were themselves uncovered of centuries of dirt, and explained, would explain all explanations... Two bone-white Gray scholars looked up from the space of floor they were methodically cleaning to watch the spurred men go through.

"Where will he be?" Younger asked.

"The King's chambers."

"The King. Has he..."

"He'll do nothing. Not yet."

"What will you tell him?"

Redhand tore off his bonnet and shook his thick hair. He pulled off his gloves and slapped them into the bonnet, gave them to Younger.

The doors of the Painted Chamber were surrounded by loafing guards who stood to some kind of attention when Redhand approached. Ignoring them, he hunched his shoulders as though disposing burdens on his back, left Younger and the redjackets at the door and went in, unannounced.

Red Senlin was there, and his two sons. The eldest was called simply Red Senlin's Son; it was he who was intimate with Young Harrah. The other Redhand had not seen at court; his name was Sennred. At Redhand's entrance the three moved around the small room as though they were counters in some game.

The Painted Chamber had been an attempt of the ancients at gentility, no doubt once very fine; but its pictured battles had long since paled to ghostly wars in a mist, where they had not been swallowed up in gray clouds of mildew. And the odd convention of having everyone, even the stricken bleeding pink guts, smile with teeth made it even more weird, remote, ungentle.

With a short nod to the sons, Redhand extended his hand to his uncle. "Welcome home."

The Great Protector Red Senlin was in this year forty-eight years old. A battle in the Outlands, where he had been King's Lieutenant, had left him one-eyed. A scarf in the Outland fashion covered the dead one; the living was cold gray. His dress was the simplest, stout country leathers long out of fashion and ridiculous on any but the very high.

Redhand's father dressed so. Before him, Redhand wore his City finery self-consciously.

Red Senlin took his hand. "Black Harrah is dead."

"Yes."

"Shot by the Just."

"Yes?"

Red Senlin withdrew his hand. Redhand knew his tone was provoking, and surely no Protector, even against his greatest enemy, would have a hated Gun used—and no one of Red Senlin's generation would have a man slain secretly. "By a Gun, nephew," he said shortly.

"These are unlovely times." Behind him, Senlin's younger son, Sennred, stirred angrily. Redhand paid a smile to the dark, close-faced boy. So different from his tall, handsome older brother, whom nothing seemed to offend—not even the attentions of Black Harrah's son.

Red Senlin mounted the single step to the painted chair and sat. "Black Harrah's estates are vast. Half the Black Downs owes him. His treason forfeits . . . much of them."

"His son . . ."

One gray eye turned to the blond boy leaning with seeming disinterest at the mantel. And back to Redhand.

"Has fled, presumably to join his father's whore and other traitors. Understand me. The King will be at liberty to dispose of much."

It was an old practice, much hated by the lesser landowners and long considered dishonorable: seize the property of one's fallen enemies to pay the friends who struck them. Redhand, after the battle at Senlinsdown, had come into valuable lands that had been Farin the Black's. He chose not to visit them; had made a present of them to Farin's wife and children. But he had kept the title "Great" that the holdings carried. And certain incomes . . . It angered Redhand now more than anything, more than not being consulted at first, more than his father's maundering about the old days, more than the compromise to his oaths to the Blacks, to be so offered a price to make his uncle King.

"The Harrahs and their Black kin will not take it well, your parceling out of their property."

"Let them take it as they must."

"You make a war between Red and Black. And whoever dies in that war, on either side, will be kin to you."

"Life," said Sennred coolly, "is not so dear as our right."

"Your—right." Somehow Sennred reminded him of his brother Younger: that same quick anger, that look as of some secret hurt.

"Must I rehearse all of that again, nephew?" Red Senlin snapped. "Black took the crown by force from King Red's son . . ."

"As you mean to do?"

"My father's father was nearest brother to King Red's son . . ."

"And Black was half-brother to King Ban himself."

"But it was my father's father who in the course of things should have been King!"

"But instead swore oaths to Black."

"Forced oaths, that . . ."

"That he swore. That my grandfather's father swore too. That you and I in turn have sworn to Black's son's son."

"Can be set aside. Your brother Learned could sway the Grays to affirm me in this."

"And forfeit all credence with the world by such deceit?"

"Deceit? I am even now Little Black's heir, in default of heirs of his flesh!"

"You know the Queen is with child."

"By Black Harrah!"

"That matters nothing to the Blacks. They will swear oaths to Little Black's child with one hand on her great belly."

"Cousin." Red Senlin's Son spoke quietly from where he lounged at the mantel. "I think I have heard all this argued before, between my father and yours. The part you take your father took often."

Redhand felt his face grow hot suddenly.

"I don't know," the Son went on lazily. "It all seems of another day to me."

"It means nothing to me either, Defender," Redhand said fiercely. "But there are others..."

"It seems to me there are prizes to be won," said the Son, cutting across Redhand more sharply now. "It seems to me that Little Black is a cold pie left over from our ancestors' feasts. My oath to him makes him taste no better to me."

"He is weak-minded," Redhand growled, not sure whether he was accusing or excusing.

"Yes," said Red Senlin's Son. "We are fallen on evil days. The King goes mad, and old oaths no longer bind." He smiled a sweet smile of complicity at Redhand, who looked away. "We are protected only by our strength." He took Redhand's arm in a sudden strong grip. "We will be King. Tell us now whether you support us in this or not."

Redhand regarded the blue, uncaring eyes. Red Senlin might be grown evil, dishonorable, gone sour in repetition of old longings; might, in a passion of vanity, betray old alliances. He might, in his passion, be slain. Might well. But this blue boy was a new thing in the world; he would never lose, because he cared for nothing. And suddenly a dark wave rose under Redhand's heart: he didn't want to be an old man yet, sitting by the fire with his father, shaking his head over the coming of evil days without honor: he wanted suddenly very much to win while he could.

"Since oaths are thrown away," he said, releasing himself from the Son's grip and stepping back to face the three of them, "why, then I won't swear, and I ask no swearing from you. Until I see no further hope in you, I am yours." Red Senlin struck the throne arm triumphantly. "But this I do swear," he went on, raising his arm against them, his voice gravelly with menace. "I am no dog of yours. And if you kick me, I will bite you to the bone."

Later, when Sennred went unasked with the Redhands to the door Defensible, Redhand could almost feel his dark mistrustful eyes.

"If we must do this thing," he said at last when they stood in the ancient rotunda, "we must at least pretend to be friends."

"I don't pretend well."

"Then you must learn." He gestured to the beetling arcades above them. "If you would live here long."

When they had gone, Sennred watched the two Gray scholars working in the long, long shafts of dusty afternoon sun at their patch of floor, dusting with delicate brushes, scraping with fine tools, copying with colored inks what they uncovered.

"A pattern."

"Part of a pattern."

Crowned men with red tears running from their eyes held hands as children's cutouts do, but each twisted in a different attitude, of joy or pain he couldn't tell, for of course they all smiled with teeth. Behind and around them, gripping them like lovers, were black figures, obscure, demons or ghosts. Each crown had burning within it a fire, and the grinning black things tore tongue and organs from this king and with them fed the fire burning in the crown of that one, tore that one's body to feed the fire burning in this one's crown, and so on around, demon and king, like a tortured circle dance.

3

"If Barnol wets the Drum with rain," sang Caredd, the Protector Redhand's wife, "then Caermon brings the Downs the same; if Caermon wets the Downs with rain, the Hub will not be dry till Fain; if Barnol leaves the Drum dry still, then...then...I forget what then."

"Each week has a name," the Visitor said.

"Each week," she said.

Barnol had wet the Drum with rain, and now, two weeks after, Caermon brought the same to Redsdown. Beyond the wide, open door of the barn, the hills, like folded hands, bare and wooded, marked with fence and harrow-cut, were curtained in silvery downpour. It whispered at the door, it ticked on the sloping roof, entered at chinks and holes, and tocked drop by drop into filling rain barrels. Safe from it in the wide, dim barn, Caredd searched for eggs in the hay that filled an old broken haywain. The Visitor followed, as he had almost continually since Fauconred had brought him there: always polite, even shy, but following anyway everywhere he was allowed, attending to her as a novice would to an ancient Gray.

"Why those names?" he asked. "What do the names mean?"

"I don't know." It was the answer she gave most often to the questions, but never impatiently. Where Fauconred would have thrown up his hands in red-faced exasperation, she merely answered, once again, "I don't know."

Caredd was more than ten years younger than her Protector husband, and seemingly as easy and fair as he was dark and troubled. Redsdown, his property, was her home, had been her father's and his father's father's—

29

he a minor Defender who had married in turn one neighbor's widow and the other's only daughter, and became thereby Protector of wide and lovely holdings. Caredd, riding as soon as she could walk, knew all its mossy woodlands and lakelets, stony uplands and wide grainfields, and loved them as she loved nothing else. She had been few other places, surely, but surely had seen nothing to compare; and she who loved the gray vacancies of the glum fortress-house caught chills in the gray vacancies of her husband's town mansion.

For sure she loved Redhand too, in her fashion. Loved him in part because he had given her her home as a wedding gift when it seemed nearly lost. Her father and brother had been ambushed on a forest road by the Just, robbed and murdered; her weak-minded mother had flirted with one malcontent Red lord after another until she had been nearly tried for treason, and her estates—beloved Redsdown—had been declared forfeit to the King: thus to Black Harrah, in fact.

And then Redhand had come. Grave, dour almost, unfailingly polite, he had wooed the disoriented, frightened tomboy with rich gifts and impatient, one-sided interviews, explaining his power at court, her mother's jeopardy—till, in a stroke of grownup wisdom, she had seen that her advantage—thus her heart—lay with him.

So there had been held in the rambling castle a grand Redhand wedding.

Of that day she remembered disjunct moments only, like tatters of a vivid dream; remembered waiting in the tiny dark vestibule before the great hall for their cue to enter, pressed tight against him, surrounded protectively by his mother, his brothers, his sweating father, how she had felt at once safe and frightened, implicated yet remote; how Mother Redhand laughed, horns called from within, butlers whispered urgently from the narrow door, and how with a full rustle of many gowns the bright knot of them had unwound into the thronged hall hung with new red banners and filled with the resinous hum of many instruments.

She remembered how the guests had dusted them with salt and wound paper thorns around their wrists, and laughed though it meant suffering would come and must be endured; and how the country people gave them candied eggs for their pillow. And she remembered when later they had taken down her hair and taken away her cloudlike gown and she had stood shyly naked before him beneath a shadow of pale lace . . .

He had stayed long enough to meet and confuse the names and faces of his new tenants, Folk she knew as dearer than relatives; and he had ridden off, to court, to battle, to his other growing properties. Except for a fidgety week or two in summer, a politic ball at Yearend, he came to Redsdown little. Sometimes she felt it might be the better way. Sometimes.

She left one speckled egg from her basketful in a dark corner for the barn elf she knew lived there. She plucked a bit of straw from her autumn-auburn hair and let the Visitor take her basket. Stone steps worn to smooth curves took them out an arched side door into a breezeway that led to the kitchen; the leaves of its black vines were already gone purple with autumn, and the rain swept across its flagged path in gusts, sticking Caredd's billowing trousers to her flank. The Visitor tried clumsily to cover her with the old cloak he still wore, but she shook him off, ran tiptoe laughing through the puddles and up the kitchen stairs, brushing the clean rain from her cheeks, laughing at the Visitor making his careful, intent way toward her.

There were great rooms at Redsdown, chill halls lined with stiff-backed benches, tree-pillared places with fireplaces large as cottages, formal rooms hung with rugs and smelling of mildew. But when there was no one to entertain, nothing to uphold, Caredd and the rest stayed in the long, smoke-blackened kitchen with the Folk. There, there were four fireplaces hung with spits, hooks and potchains, with high-backed settles near and chimney corners always warm; there were thick tables worn so the smooth grain stood out, piled high with autumn roots to be strung or netted and hung from the black beams above. The rain tapped and cried at the deep small windows but couldn't come in.

Two ancient widows sat making thread in a corner, one of them meanwhile rocking ever with her naked foot a bagcradle hung there in the warmth. "If Barnol wets the Drum with rain," they sang, "then Caermon brings the Downs the same..."

"Rain indeed," said the Defender Fauconred from within his settle. He dipped a wooden ladle into a kettle steaming on the hob and refreshed his cup. "And when will it stop, ladies?"

"Could be tonight, Defender," said one, turning her distaff.

"Could be tomorrow," said the other, turning hers.

"Could turn to snow."

"Could continue wet."

Fauconred grunted and filled the cup of Mother Caredd, who took it with a slow, abstracted graciousness, set it on the settle-arm, and began to put up her cloudy white hair with many bone pins. It seemed that Mother Caredd's hair always needed putting up; Caredd rarely saw her but she was piling up, endlessly, patiently, its never-cut length.

"Now you see, Visitor," she said absently, "those are rainy-sounding names for weeks, is all; Barnol and Caermon, Haspen and Shen... like Doth is dry and Finn is cold..."

"I wondered about their origin," the Visitor said. He sat next to Caredd, looking from one speaker to the next as though in a schoolroom, teacher or pupil or both. Mother Caredd had no more lesson to say, and shrugged and smiled. The unhappy end of her playing at politics had left her vaguer even than she had always been, but also somehow calmer, more lovely, and gently accepting; where the Visitor disturbed and perplexed Fauconred, and fascinated Caredd, Mother Caredd just smiled at him, as though his dropping from heaven were the most natural of things.

"For any real answers," Caredd said, "you'll have to go to the Grays, in the end. For all old knowledge."

"They know?"

"They say they know. Help me here." She was trying with her long patient fingers to restring an old carved instrument.

"They say," Mother Caredd went on as though to herself, "that all the Just have names for their names. Is that so? Naming their names, and why... Their Guns have names too, all of them, don't they? I wonder if the Guns' names have names, and so on and on..."

"I don't know, Mother," Caredd said, laughing. "Could they remember all that?"

"I couldn't. But I wouldn't want to, would I?"

Caredd loved her mother fiercely, and though she allowed herself to smile at her rambling chatter, she let none mock her, and would die to keep her from being hurt again.

"The Just," the Visitor said, nodding; these he knew; but after a moment asked: "Who are they? How would I know them?"

"Murderers," Caredd answered simply. "These keys are warped."

"Bandits, as I told you," Fauconred said, frowning into his cup. "The men, without law or honor; the women, whores."

"Madmen," said Mother Caredd.

"Why Just, then?" the Visitor asked Caredd.

"A name from longer ago than anyone remembers. Perhaps the name had a meaning. It's said they're dreamers." She plucked a dampened note. "Nightmare dreamers."

"Old names persist," Fauconred said. "Like Protector, Defender. Protectors and Defenders of the Folk, anciently."

"Protectors of the Folk against . . ."

Fauconred knitted his gray brows. "Why, against the Just, I suppose."

Caredd strummed a tuneless tune and put down the ancient instrument. The two widows went on spinning their eternal thread. "If it snows on Yearend Day," they sang, "then snow and rain will fall till Fain/Brings the New Year round again . . ."

By evening, the rain had blown away toward the City, leaving only a rent sash of clouds for the sun to color as it set. To watch, Caredd had climbed a hundred stairs to the long, fanged battlement that guarded Redsdown's Outward side, and then up between two broken castellations to where she knew of a flat, private place to sit. On the tower behind her, two forked banners, sunset-red, snapped tirelessly in rhythm with her own heavy cloak's blowing. She pulled it tighter around her, drew her knees up, wondered what Redhand was about tonight . . . There was a polite, introductory sort of noise on the battlement below. Caredd smiled down at the tireless Visitor.

"Even here?" she asked. "Those steps are long."

"I'm sorry," said the Visitor. "I'll go back."

"No. Stay. Better to talk to you than . . . Stay."

"I was wondering," he began, and Caredd laughed. He put his head down and went on carefully. "Wondering why no one of the Folk will talk with me." He had gone about the farms with Caredd, watching her stop everywhere to hug and talk and fondle babies, be cooed over herself by old ones who treated her as something between a cherished pet and a princess. But their happy chatter had ceased before him, turned to a cool reserve; he had never had any yield him anything but a nod and a wary, almost frightened smile.

"They think you are a creature of the Grays," Caredd said simply.

"A . . . creature?"

"Of old, the Grays could make combatants against the Seven Possessors. Creatures not anything but one of the Seven Strengths. The Folk have a thousand stories about such things, battles of the Seven Possessors against the Seven Strengths. Moral stories, you know; Gray knowledge or teaching made into a story about a battle. The Folk take them for real, the Sevens, real enough to see with eyes and touch."

"But the Gray in the village—he's just as afraid of me."

Caredd laughed again. "Old Driggory? He's afraid that you might have been sent to do battle against his own Possessor, the one named Blem." The Visitor looked puzzled. "Drunkenness. A good old man Driggory is, but a simple country clerk; he'd hardly know what the great Grays are capable of. Because it's from him, you see, and all his cousins, the village clerks and little Grays, that the Folk have learned their tales of the Sevens, from long ago."

The Visitor shook his head. "I wanted to talk with them. How can I explain I am no creature of the Grays?"

Caredd looked down at the strange personage below her, who looked up with his infinite blank eyes. Indeed, if there were Gray champions of the Right, they might look like this: or then Demons too. "Whose creature are you?" she asked.

The Deep had drunk the sun once more, and though the clouds Outward weren't yet drained of all color, the sky above had been swept clean of cloud, and on that blue-black ceiling already burned three of the Wanderers, pink, gold and red, all decrescent. "I can't remember," the Visitor said, as though for the first time.

"Perhaps," said Caredd, "you are no Strength, but Possessed; and the Possessor has eaten your memory and made your hair fall out. The Possessor Blem can do that; they show it in the pageants at Yearend." She was a wind-blown silhouette in the crack of battlement, and the Visitor couldn't see her little mocking smile.

"And if I am?" said the Visitor. "I don't think I am, but if I am?"

"If you are," Caredd said thoughtfully. "Well. I wouldn't know what then, and neither would Driggory. You'd have to go to Inviolable and ask."

"Inviolable?"

"The Grays' house in the mountains. Or"—a sudden thought that made her smile again—"wait till Fauconred takes you to my husband. His brother is a great Gray, oh very high." She would like to see Learned's unstirrable face, when this creature asked wisdom of him.

The Visitor turned his bald face to the deep sky he knew had made him. Had made him for—somewhere within him some formed thing tried to coalesce: a reason, a direction, the proper question, the name uncoded. He stood stock-still and watched it light up fitfully the structured regularity of his manufacture... and then dissolve as quickly into blank unknowing again.

"Very well," he said, when he was sure it was gone. "I'll wait, then. A little longer."

Learned Redhand was not particularly learned, though he was for sure Redhand. His family name had hardly hindered his quick rise through many degrees to the gray he wore, dark as rainclouds about to break; but still, it was due as much to his own efforts, to his subtlety if not depth of mind, to his unflappable grace of manner. Despite a certain cynicism in him, a smiling disregard for the dogmas of his Order that unsettled people, he had a deep affection for the elaborate systems, framed in ritual as though in antique, lustrous wood, that had taken the Grays countless centuries to create. But he had little interest in mastering those systems in all their complexity; was content to float on the deep stream of Gray knowledge, trailing one finger, buoyed by the immunity a Gray's unarmed strength gave him in the violent world of the court.

He did love without reservation, though, the house Inviolable, where he had first put on white linen, where he had grown up in the Grays and gained whatever wisdom he possessed. He loved the fang of mountain Inviolable had held since before any but they could remember, that looked down on the far-off City and Outward to the Downs, surrounded by the sounds and silence of sweet rocky woods. And he loved above all the ancient garden closed within its walls. Tended and nursed over centuries, its shadowed groves, vined walls, and sudden fountains had become a system of private places, singular yet unified, like states of mind.

The year was late now in the garden, that was its mood. The dark groves were mostly unleaved, and the intersecting paths were deep-strewn with black and brown. The air was clear and windy; the wind gathered leaves and the voices of distant boys at play, blew rippling waves through the coppery ivy, white-flecked the many fountains with foam.

How cold it must be now on the Drum, Learned Redhand thought, when even these fountains are blown black and gray . . . It had been some years now since he had had need to come back to Inviolable, and as he waited now in the garden for the interview he had asked for, he felt himself given over to an unaccustomed sweet nostalgia, a multiple sense of self and season, composed like a complex harmony out of the afternoon, the garden, the fountains—and himself, a boy, a man, in this same season but other years, with other selves in the same skin. It made him feel unreal, rich yet illusory.

The narrow, flinty archway that led into Inviolable from the garden, high as ten men, had neither door nor gate, only a great black drape of some ancient, everlasting stuff, so heavy that the restless air could barely lift it; it rose a bit and fell with a low solemn snap of one edge, filled again with breath and exhaled slowly. Learned

watched go in and out of this door young scholars and
country clerks in bone-white robes; smoky-gray lawyers
and iron-gray lesser judges followed by white-robed
boys carrying writing cases; thunder-gray court minis-
ters and chamberlains with their lay petitioners . . . And
then he stood as one came out, diminutive, and smaller
still with age, in gray indistinguishable from black and
little different from an old widow's black cowl, unac-
companied save for a thick cane. They stood aside on
the steps for this shabby one, who nodded smiling side
to side. Learned Redhand rose, but was waved away
when he offered help; he made a graceful obeisance
instead. The old, old Arbiter of all right and wrong, the
grayest of all Grays, sat down on Learned's bench with
care.

"It's not too cold, here in the garden?" Learned
Redhand inquired.

"No, Learned, if you be brief." There was little about
the Arbiter Mariadn that revealed gender, except the
voice; all else had grown sexless with great age, but the
voice somehow was still the young Downs farm girl she
had been sixty years ago. "But before we speak, you
must remove that." Her index, slim as bone, pointed to
the bit of red ribbon Learned Redhand wore.

He knew better than to fence with the Arbiter. As
though it were his own idea, he detached it and pocketed
it even as he spoke: "I come to ask you to clarify for me
a bit of ancient history," he said.

"You were ever nice in talk, Redhand," Mariadn said.
"Be plainer. Your faction—I'm sorry, your family's faction—
wishes the oath sworn to the Blacks set aside."

"The Protectorate wish it."

"Yes?"

"It's complex," Learned said thoughtfully, as though
considering the merits of the argument. "By all the old
laws of inheritance, it seems Red Senlin's grandfather
should have been King. In acknowledgment of those
claims, he was named heir to Little Black. Now the

Black faction seems ready to discredit the claim on the grounds that the Queen is with child, though none believes the King capable of such a thing after ten barren years of marriage. The Reds seem ready to force Red Senlin's claim, and crown him now in repayment for the Blacks' reneging."

"As a matter of principle, I suppose," said the Arbiter coolly. "Just to set the record straight."

Learned Redhand smiled. "Arbiter, there is doubtless much to be won. Little Black's reign has been long and dishonorable. The Red Protectorate suffered much from Black Harrah's ministry; I think they surely wish revenge. No. Not a matter of principle. The reverse."

"And they come then beforehand to have their hands washed at our fountain. Why should we be muddied by their revenge?"

Learned paused, looking into a pale, slate-colored agate he wore on one finger. The expert at circumlocution must first have his matter clear to himself: but when it was clear, he found no pretty way to say it. "Arbiter: Red Senlin means to be King. Many of the great support him in this. Even to war with the Queen. They wish their enterprise sanctioned by the Grays."

"And if we cannot sanction it? They must not ask for arbitration, Learned, unless they mean to abide by it."

"That's the hardest thing." He turned and turned the stone on his forefinger. "I needn't preach to you that the strong chain of oaths seems barely a thread in these bad times. But I feel sure that if the Grays decide against Red Senlin, the Reds ... will lose adherents, yes. Will lose credence in the eyes of the Folk. Will give pretexts even to the Just, who grow strong lately. But will proceed, anyway."

Too old in judgment to be indignant, Mariadn considered, her eyes closed. "And will perhaps then be beaten by the Queen, and all hanged, and their sin made plain."

"Perhaps. But I think not. Black Harrah is dead. And

the Great Protector Redhand and all his adherents are with Red Senlin."

"Dindred possesses them," the Arbiter said quietly. "Pride is their master, and what Strength can be called against him?"

"Arbiter," said Learned Redhand more urgently, "the question of succession is surely doubtful. It could be settled reasonably two ways; surely there is much in law to be said for the Senlin claim. But consider further the Order we owe. I think Red Senlin, without our help, has even chances of doing this thing. With a Gray word behind him, the thing is nearly certain. If he has our judgment and wins, we are the stronger for it. If without our judgment, then our judgment will have little power hence."

"The power of our judgment is in its Righteousness."

"Yes. Of old. And we must take care for that power. It is threatened. The Just speak Leviathan's name in the villages this year again. If the Protectorate act in disregard of us, then . . . then oaths far older than the Protectorate's to Little Black's kin are weakened, and begin to pass away."

The Arbiter Mariadn covered her old eyes with the long fingers of one hand. Only her finely lined mouth was visible; her voice held Learned Redhand like the gentlest of vices. "Learned. I am old. I see few visitors. Perhaps I can't any longer grasp the world's complexities: no, not these new heresies, I hate and fear them, so I am not qualified to speak. I must lean on you, on your worldliness, which I partly fear too . . . Only swear to me now, Learned, on all the ancient holy things there are, that what you advise you advise out of love and care for our Order. For our Order only."

"I do so swear," Learned said without hesitation. Mariadn breathed a little sigh, rose and took up her cane. She started slowly back toward the black-hung doorway into Inviolable.

"So," she said, not looking back. "It shall be as you

advise, if I can sway others. And perhaps, after all, it's . . . only a little sin. Perhaps."

Learned Redhand sat a long time after she had gone, in the gathering evening, watching black leaves fall and float in the restless pool of the fountain. He should be in his carriage, taking news of his success to the Harbor: but it was success he suddenly felt little desire to announce.

Strange, he thought; she and he had talked so much of the new, oath-breaking way of the world, and yet when he swore to her, she accepted it unhesitatingly. It was inconceivable to her that he, a Gray, in no matter how disastrous a day, could swear falsely.

Perhaps indeed he hadn't. Without the Grays, Learned Redhand would be someone else's younger brother, nothing more, the Grays' strength and health were his. In any case, soon or late, there would be a testing of that oath, a reckoning. He wondered how he would bear.

He rose to go. The autumn evening had grown dense; the great age of the garden seemed to him suddenly palpable, and deeply melancholy.

Haspensweek Eve, and suddenly cold even in the City in its cup of mountains. That night they moved King Little Black from the Citadel to an old Black mansion, long shuttered, that sat inaccessible on a finger of rock, called Sping, just outside the High City gates.

For it had been decided, in a Whole-meeting of the Protectorate, that Red Senlin was Little Black's heir, and Viceroy too in times of the King's madness. The Black lords, of course, had stayed away from the meeting; so had many others. And even the Reds and Folk ombudsmen who had come, mostly dependents of Senlin's and Redhand's, were so glum and silent that Red Senlin had ended his brief screaming insults and arguments,

his shouts echoing in the near-empty rotunda. No
matter; It had been decided.

The small cavalcade, shielded by armed men, moved
through the shadowed dark of the thousand-faced street.
It had been decided that the King was indeed in his
madness now, and for sure looked at least sickly and
weak. He huddled on his nag, folded up in an old black
cloak, and looked apprehensively from the silent crowd
to the gleam of axes and spears, the smoky, flaring
torches of his escort.

The Viceroy Red Senlin rode with his golden Son. It
had been decided that the Son and his younger brother,
dark Sennred, with a number of adherents, should ride
toward Senlinsdown and rally there all the Protector's
friends. Young Harrah, the Viceroy had learned, had
gone off in quite another direction, toward the Black
Downs and the Queen.

Redhand rode on the King's right side; on his left
rode Redhand's father, Old Redhand. Around Old
Redhand's neck hung an ancient chain, giltwork once,
now worn again to the naked iron, that had ever been
the sign of the chiefest of the vast Redhand clan. From
this old chain hung now something new: the great
carved beryl that is the City's seal, borne by the King's
lieutenant, Master of the City—until recently, Black
Harrah.

It had been decided that the family Redhand should
inherit that rich honor.

It had been more than deference in Redhand that
had insisted that not he but his father be given the City
seal. Redhand knew that war with the Queen would
come quick as anger, and he had hoped that the City
seal would keep his father safe in the City while he and
Red Senlin acted out the treasonous show they had
trumped up together against the old man's wishes. But
it hadn't worked. It had been instead decided—by Old
Redhand, decided with all his remaining strength and
will—that in case of sudden need the seal would de-

volve upon his son, and he, Old Redhand, would take command of the Redhand arms. He wasn't too old to fight for his friend.

Redhand tried to keep his eyes on the street, on the King, on the faces of the crowd—but they were drawn by his father's face. It was a face marked like a cliffside by wind and time, harder than his steel, and not softened by the halo of sparse hair he wore in the old fashion cropped close around his ears. His eyes, unlike his son's, were drawn to nothing, but looked ahead, farther than the end of the street or the end of the world.

When they passed through Farinsgate and out onto the Heights outside the City walls, the crowd became thinner. It wasn't a time for High City people to be outside their gates. The great mansions of this side, Farin's House, Blackharbor, were dark; only one house was lit, there, at the causeway's end, on the rock Sping, lit by the torches and watchfires of those assigned to guard close forever the little King.

Suddenly Old Redhand stopped his horse. Someone was pushing his way into the ranks ahead; the Viceroy Red Senlin leaned out to hear his news. A murmur went up from the armed men. Someone whispered to the King, and a pale smile grew on his face. Younger worked his horse to Redhand's side and told him the news.

The Queen had gathered an army on the Drumskin. She had turned Inward, had ceased to flee since none pursued, and unless a large force met her soon there was nothing to prevent her laying siege to the City itself. It hadn't happened in time out of mind. The Queen, seemingly, intended it.

Old Redhand, with only half a glance at his son, spurred forward to where Red Senlin summoned him.

It meant battle, and there was much to decide.

4

All day since before chill dawn the red-jacketed riders
with their striped packs had come down the water-stairs
toward the lake, guiding their mounts along the horse
ramps. Shouted orders carried far in the still, cold air;
captains perspired despite the frost steaming from their
bellowing mouths. Great straining pulleys lowered painted
wagons toward the ferries; horses reared and laughed;
harried ostlers attempted to count off from lists, screaming at the watermen, whom no fee could hurry.

The girl had pulled and hauled since morning, somehow intensely elated by the first winey wrong-way
breezes of the year; now the hard sunlight cast unaccustomed glitter on the stirred waters and heated her
shorn blond head. She laughed out loud to see them
struggle with their war there on the bank. Her laugh
was lost in the uproar; whips snapped, and the oxen on
the far bank lowed in misery as they began to turn the
creaking winches once again.

Soldiers sitting atop piled bundles above her called
down pleasant obscenities as she pushed to the forward
end of the laden barge. She climbed up a crate that had
Redhand's open-palm sign on it in new red paint, and,
shielding her eyes, looked up to where the four tongues
of bridges came out of the High City's gate-mouths.
She thought probably there, at the gate called Goforth,
the generals would come out—yes, there, for now, as
she looked, their banners all burst forth from the
Citadel onto the bridge-stairs, as though a giant had
blown out from the gate a handful of petals. She
couldn't see faces, but for sure they must be there, for
there was Redhand's open palm, and the dried-blood

red of Senlin marked with ancient words; the soldiers
and the City cheered them, and she cheered too,
laughing at the thought that the bridge might break
under their great weight of pride and drop them,
leaving their banners only, light as wind.

Something colder than his cold armor took hold on
Redhand's heart, there where he stood among the gay
flags with his brother Younger. Through Goforth his
father, Old Redhand, with harsh pulls at the reins,
forced his warhorse Dark Night. Through the cloud of
banners before the gate, through the ribboned throng
of riders, hearing no salutations, up to where his sons
stood.

"Is our House all here?" he said, and then said again,
over the great-throated war viols' endless chants.

"Yes," Redhand answered him. "Father . . ."

"Then give me the baton."

So many things, hurtful or too grownup for the child,
had Redhand ever given up to his father: but never
with such black presage, too cold for anger, as now
when he lifted the slim general's stick to his father's
outstretched hand.

"You can still stay," he growled. Both their hands
held the baton. "Stay and see to the City . . ."

"You see to it," his father said. "Give it to me."

Redhand released it; Old Redhand tucked it into his
sash and leaned out toward Younger, whose look clung
desperately to his father's face. Old Redhand pulled
Younger to him with a mailed hand, kissed him. He
kissed him again, slapped his cheek lightly without
word or smile. Turned away and tore from his old neck
the Redhand chain with the City seal hung from it.

"Senlin!" he called out in a voice not his own. Red
Senlin stood in his stirrups and waved to him. "Would
you be *King*?" Red Senlin drew his sword, pointed
Outward. Old Redhand turned to Redhand his son. He

tossed him the chain. "Take care," he said. "Watch well."

Too proud to dismount to cross the two generals walked their heavy steeds with infinite care over the swaying bridge. Redhand watched their exertions till he could bear no more, and ran, his heart full, up the stairs, through Goforth, into the silent City that the chain he held made him master of.

That evening the first light snow was dusting Redsdown, blown in from the Drum. From a window in the high headland tower that marked Redsdown's edge, Caredd and her mother watched the Protectors' horses, and Fauconred and his redjackets, and the horsegatherers, and the Visitor too, gather on the rutted road toward the mountains and the far-off City. They were dim in the gusts of fine blown snow; there was the Visitor in his brown Endwife's cloak. The horsegatherers flicked their lashes, and the company unwound, their sharp hooves loud on the new-frozen ground.

"See how he drives them," Mother Caredd said.

"Fauconred?" Caredd asked.

"Yes, he is driven too."

"Who drives them, Mother?"

"Why, Rizna, Daughter," said her mother. "Surely you see him there, so tall, with his black eye sockets, and the sickle hung on his neck . . . See how he makes them step along!"

"Mother . . ."

"Like some great raggedy shepherd driving silly sheep . . . What great steps he takes!"

"Mother, there's no such thing there." Yet she looked hard, holding her throat where the blood beat.

"Why does he drive them, where, for what? See them look back, and then ride on for fear . . ."

"There's nothing there, Mother! Stop!" She strained to see the caravan, strung out along the road; they were shadows already, and then disappeared in a mist of

blown snow. Mother Caredd began to put up her hair
with many bone pins...

If snow fell heavily in the mountains as they went up
the high road Cityward, they would be delayed till long
after Yearend, holed up in some bleak lodge or pilgrim
house of the Grays, and Fauconred didn't want that at
all. He hurried as fast as he could through the black,
leafless forest, had men ride ahead and behind to
watch for the Just: these mountains were their castles
and cities, they knew the rocky highlands and had a
name for every thick ravine, could appear and disappear in them like the dream faces Fauconred saw in the
knotted treeboles. He harried his riders till he was
hoarse with it, and would have pushed them on through
the nights, if he hadn't feared breaking some valued leg
or his own neck in the dark even more than he feared
the sounds and silence beyond the vague, smoky hole
his campfires made.

He told himself, he told his men, that what made
him afraid was ambush, the Guns of the Just. But the
horsegatherers, Drumskin men, had their own tales of
these mountain forests, and told them endlessly around
the fire: stories of the Hollowed. "My grandfather's
half-brother was taking horses to the City once, on this
same road, and saw a thing, about dawn, running along
beside the road, in the trees, making no sound, a
thing—a thing as fearful as if you saw a great hooded
cloak stand up and walk with no one in it, my grandfather's half-brother said..." The Hollowed, they said,
were the bodies of the Possessors, abandoned by the
Possessors themselves to their own malignant dead
wanderings when the Strengths had driven the Possessors from the homeplaces of men into the Deep. Here
the bodies wandered, Hollowed, unable to rest, empty
cups still holding the dregs of poison, drinking up what
souls they could seize on to sustain them, insect, animal, man.

Most days now they could see, far and dim, higher

than any reaching crag, Inviolable in its high seat, placid and strong; even thought they heard, one cold still day, its low bells ring. But then they turned a twisting mile down the valley, between two high naked rocks men called the Knees, and the weather grew enough warmer to raise thick, bitter fogs; Inviolable was lost. By dawn on Lowday, the day before Yearend, the day of the Possessors' Eve, they were deep in the river Wanderer's rocky home.

Somewhere below their narrow way, Wanderer chased herself noisily through her halls, echoing in flumes and gorges, spitting at cave-mouths; but they could see nothing of her, for her breath was white and dense almost as haysmoke, and cold as Finn.

Fauconred wouldn't stop. It was baffling and frightening to try to pass this way in a fog, and hurry too, with the river's roar filling up your head; but it was worse to stop, so that the horses, stuck on a ledge, might panic and leap. It took all his strength and lungs to force them further down, to where at last the high wall beside them broke and a pass led down away, high-sided, obscure, but a pass: the Throat they called it, and it spoke with Wanderer's great voice even as it swallowed them. The Throat took away their own voices too, when they were inside it, amplified them in a weird way, so that every man who spoke looked behind him with a start for the source of his own words.

It was the Visitor, whose ears had proved sharp as a dog's, who first heard the other horsemen in the pass.

"It's only the Throat," Fauconred said, "our own hooves echoing."

"No. Make them stop, and listen. Down there, coming up."

Fauconred tried to read an imagining fear in the Visitor's face, but there was only attention. The fear was his own. He shouted a halt, and the horsegatherers sang out to still the herd. Then they waited for their own echoes to cease.

It was there, the noise of someone somewhere. The Visitor said ahead, Fauconred said behind, the horse-gatherers and guard stared wildly here and there, their panic spreading to the horses and confusing every ear. Mist drawn into the Throat went by in ragged cloaks to hide and then reveal them to each other. And then they saw, far down the Throat, gray shapes moving at a mad pace toward them, gesticulating, pale as smoke.

A rasp of steel unsheathing. Fauconred knew that if they were men, they must be charged, hard, for he could not be forced back through the Throat and live. If they were not men... He shouted his redjackets forward and charged hard, hoping they dared follow.

The pale riders drew closer, coalescing out of fog and thunder of hooves. For sure they were men, yes, living men—were—were a war party, arms drawn, were a Red party—Redhand! "Redhand!" he shouted, and twisted his mount hard. They nearly collided. Fauconred just managed to keep his riders from tangling with his master's. He turned to laugh with Redhand out of relief, and looked into his face, a gray, frightening mask, eyes wide and mad. "Redhand..." He seemed a man, yet as Fauconred watched him stare around him unseeing, drawn sword clutched tight, he felt a chill of fear: Hollowed... some dream shape they could take...

The form Redhand spoke. "Turn your men." The harsh voice was an exhausted croak, expressionless. "Make for the Outward road."

Fauconred saw the iron chain of the Redhands hung on his neck. "What's happened?"

"War with the Queen."

"Red Senlin..."

"Slain. Slain before Forgetful... Why don't you turn?" he asked without inflection. Someone came up suddenly beside Fauconred, and Redhand flung out his sword arm with a cry: "Who is it... what..."

"The one I sent to tell you of. The... Visitor."

"Keep him for right's sake from me!..." The Visitor

drew back, but Redhand's wide eyes still fixed him.
Fauconred thought to speak, did not. There was a
moment of freak silence in the Throat, and Redhand
burst into strange, racking sobs.

He hadn't slept in days, had pressed every man he
could into service, had flung them through the forest
without mercy, once turning rebellious laggards at sword-
point... Fauconred, taking command reluctantly, coaxed
them all back through the Throat the way Redhand had
come, had camp made and a precious cask broached,
that calmed anger and fear both: and while Blem had
his say, Drink-up, Sleep-fast, No-tomorrow, Fauconred
drew from his master the tale, in words drunk with
weariness and grief.

The Queen had led the Red army a quickwing chase
across the plains toward the barren Drumsedge, Red
Senlin desperately trying to cut her off from the Inward
roads and her Outward strength both, until, weary with
chase and no battle, he had made for Forgetful, watch
castle of the Edge, where the garrison owed him. They
had reached it Finnsweek Eve. They struck a truce
with the Queen to last over Yearend. And then some of
Red Senlin's men had been out foraging and been
attacked by a marauding party of the enemy. Old
Redhand and Red Senlin had issued from the castle to
help—and been boxed by the mass of the Queen's
army, who had thus drawn them out.

Red Senlin was among the first killed. Old Redhand
had been killed or captured, none knew, none could tell
him...

For two days Redhand had stayed in the Harbor in an
agony of fear. And then another messenger arrived, a
boy gaunt with cold and hunger, the red palm sign on
his shoulder.

Old Redhand had been captured in the battle and
imprisoned in Forgetful's belly where the day before he
had been guest. Next day in the first light the boy

watched them take him out into the courtyard, where snow fell; and a bastard son of Farin the Black chopped off his head with a sword.

The boy had fled then. He knew only that Young Harrah would be master at Forgetful, and that the Queen came Inward, behind him, with her army.

"They will be at the margin of the Downs tomorrow," Redhand said. "Red Senlin's Son is marching from Senlinsdown to stop her; we must go on, we must march before night . . ." He tried to rise, but Fauconred restrained him gently.

"Sleep," he said. "Sleep awhile."

Redhand slept.

They made a crown for Red Senlin of paper, and put it on his head; put the head on a pole and carried it before them as they streamed Inward across the Drum. Old Redhand they left in the courtyard of Forgetful where Young Harrah, its master now, could bury him or not, as he chose; but Red Senlin went before the Queen's army.

The immense, dull armor the Queen had had made for herself, wide-winged and endlessly riveted, crossed with chains and bristling with points, would have seemed comical if it hadn't first seemed so cruel. It took a great laborer of a stallion to bear both it and the Queen; her captain had paid high for it after she had ridden to death the strong black she had fled on. Beneath her visor, above the heavy veil she wore against the cold, her eyes, lampblack-soft and dark, made it seem that somewhere amid the massive flesh and unyielding armor a beautiful woman was held captive. It had been, at times, a useful illusion.

It had been Black Harrah who, ten years before, partly as a useful diplomacy, partly as a tool for his own use, and partly as a joke on the tiny weak-headed King, had brought back from the fastness of the Outlands the hulking, black-eyed girl, chieftain's daughter in a thousand brass spangles. Her bride-price, her own vast weight in precious metals, had made her father a rich man indeed.

And now Black Harrah is dead, slain she is sure by the Reds; and she, from ceaseless chase and fight, has miscarried his child in anguish: though none yet knows it. So at sunset near the Little Lake, those dark eyes look out on a thin line of Red horse and foot, Redhand's, Red Senlin's Son's; she thinks of them slain, and her armed feet in their blood.

Her enemies had come together at the crossroads beyond Senlinsdown. There they made a crown for Red Senlin's Son, a circle of gold riveted to his helmet, and Redhand put it on his head, and their two armies made a cheer muffled in Drumwind and cold; and they mounted again and rode for the Little Lake. At sunset they flew down the Harran road through the still, white Downs, Redhand's fast horsemen the vanguard, and Red Senlin's younger son Sennred fierce with grief. Lights were being lit in the last few cottages snowed in amid the folded land; sheep stamped and steamed, and ran huddling quick to bier as they passed.

They came down between the milestones onto the frozen Drum again as the sun began to move into the smoky Deep ahead; the Queen, expecting them, had drawn up in the crisp snow before the Little Lake, and set her trophy there. When his sons see it, it is a week frozen, the flesh picked at by wind, the jaw fallen away.

They look toward each other there, and the scouts and captains point out which is which. The Queen on her stallion. Kyr, her cold Outland chief. Red Senlin's Son, tallest of his army. There, by the Dog banner, Sennred small and bent. Redhand—yes, she knows Redhand. Red Senlin's Son looks for someone, some banner, doesn't find it. They look a long time. The last sun makes them pieces in a game: the Queen's a black silhouette army, the King Red Senlin's Son's touched with crimson. They turn away.

The game is set. The first moves come at dawn.

How the word moved, that brought to a wind-licked
flat above the battle plain so many of the brown sister-
hood, the Endwives, none knows but they. But they
have come; in the morning they are there, they have
walked through the night or driven their two-wheeled
carts or long tent-wagons; and they have come in
numbers. For as long as any alive remembers, war with
the Just has been harry and feint, chase and evade,
search and skirmish, and tangle only at the last bitter
moment. Now the Endwives look down through the
misty dawn at two armies, Protectors and Defenders
and all their banners, hundreds to a side, flanked by
snowbound cavalry, pushing through the drifts toward
each other as though to all embrace.

"Who is that so huge on a cart horse, sister?"

"The Queen. Her enemy's head is her standard. See
how she comes to the front . . ."

Redhand would not have the Visitor near him.
Fauconred, knowing nothing better to do, has sent him
to the Endwives to help. He stands with them, watching,
listening.

"It'll snow again soon. It's darker now than at dawn."

"The wind blows toward the Queen."

"Whose is the Dog banner? They fall back from him."

"Sennred, the new King's stoop-shouldered brother
. . . Ay, the murder they make."

Toward noon the snow does begin; the wind is Outward, blowing toward the Queen, who must fall back.
The shifting line of their embrace wavers, moves toward the lake, then away, then closer; then the Queen's
ranks part, here, there, and many are forced into the
black water. If she had hoped fear of that frozen lake
would keep her army from breaking, she was wrong; it
looks a cruel gamble to the sisters; but then the wind
and snow darken the field, put out the sun, and the
Endwives listen, silent, to screams, cries, and the clash
of metal so continuous as to be a steady whisper,

drowned out when the wind cries or the Drum speaks
with horse-sortie.

"Feed the fires, sisters. Keep torches dry. They make
a long night for us here."

"Fall back!" And they do fall back, released from the
maelstrom by his harsh croak, echoed by his captains;
only Sennred and his wing hesitate, Sennred still eager.
But they fall back.

"Regroup!" They force their panting mounts into a
semblance of order behind him, the twisting hooves
throwing up great clots of muddy snow. His red-palm
banner is obscure in the snowy dark; but they see his
snow-washed sword. His arm feels like an arm of stone:
that numb, that obdurate. "Now on! Strike! Fall on
them there!" and the force, in a churning, swirling
storm of mud, beat the Drum.

He is outpaced by Sennred, is cut off by a flanking
movement of near-spent horse, the stone arm flails with
a stone will of its own; he can hear nothing but a great
roar and the screaming of his own breath. Then the
Black horses part, shattered, and fall away. The tireless
snowstorm parts also, and the field grows for a moment
ghastly bright, and he sees, amid the broken, fleeing
Black cavalry, the Queen, shuffling away on her big
horse, slim sword in her great mailed hand.

He shouts forward whoever is around him; the sight
of her lashes through him, an icy restorative. Horror
and hate, he would smash her like a great bug if he
could. He flings from his path with a kind of joy some
household people of hers, sees her glance back at him
and his men, sees her urge the horse into a massive
trot: does not see, in his single purpose, her man Kyr
and his Outland spear racing for him. Someone shouts
behind him; he wheels, suddenly breathless with the
shock of collision; his horse screams under him, for the
stone arm with its own eye has seen and struck, throwing the spear's point into his horse's breast. She leaps,

turns in air spurting blood, catapulting Kyr away by the spear driven in her, falls, is overrun by Kyr's maddened horse, whose hooves trample her screaming head, trample her master, Redhand. He is kicked free, falls face down. His flung sword, plunged in mud, waves, trembles, is still. Redhand is still.

Blood frozen quickly stays as bright as when shed.

The Endwives, intent as carrion birds, move among the fallen, choosing work, turning over the dead to find the living caught beneath.

The Visitor's manufacture keeps him from weariness, but not from horror. He hears its cries in his ears, he stumbles over it half buried in bloody snow. His eyes grow wide with it.

His difficulty is in telling the living from the dead. Some still moving he sees the sisters examine and leave; others who are unmoving they minister to. This one: face down, arm twisted grotesquely; well... the Visitor turns him gently with more than man's strength, holds his torch near to see. "You're dead." A guess. The eyes look up at him unseeing. "Are you dead?" He wipes pink snow from the face: it is the man Redhand, who begins to breathe stertorously, and blows a blood-bubble from his gray lips. The Visitor considers this sufficient and lifts him easily in his arms, turning this way and that to decide what next. Redhand's breath grows less labored; he clings to the Visitor almost like a child in nurse's arms, his numb fingers clutching the brown cloak. Fauconred's tent: he sees its Cup banner far off as someone passes it with a torch. Even when it disappears into darkness again, he moves unerringly toward it, through that trampled, screaming field: and each separate cry is separately engraved on a deathless, forgetless memory.

Fauconred starts to see him. His day has been full of terrible things, but somehow, now, the Visitor's face seems most terrible: what had seemed changeless and blank has altered, the eyes are wide and deep-shadowed, the mouth thin and down-drawn.

"It's he, Redhand." The smooth, cool voice has not changed. "Help me. Tell me if he's dead. Tell me . . . He mustn't be dead. He mustn't be. He must live."

TWO

■

SECRETARY

1

An image of Caermon: a man, crowned with leaves, holding in one hand a bunch of twigs, and seated on a stone.

He found that though he came no closer to any Reason or Direction in his being, his understanding of his faculties grew, chiefly through the amazement of others. Fauconred had first noticed his hearing, in the Throat; his strength in lifting and carrying wounded Redhand had amazed the Endwives. Now Learned Redhand had observed him learn to read the modern and ancient languages in mere weeks—and remember everything he learned in them.

An image of Shen: a woman, weeping, seated in a cart drawn by dogs, wearing a crown.

The Visitor measured his growth in more subtle things: when he saw the King Red Senlin's Son, his head low, sword across his lap, attention elsewhere, he felt still the strength in him, no less than on the field. It gave him an odd thrill of continuity, a pleasurable sense of understanding: the King on the battlefield or here at his ease is one King. When the Visitor tried to describe the experience to Learned Redhand, the Gray failed to

grasp what was marvelous in it. He found it much more
compelling that the Visitor could cause a stone thrown
into the air to float slowly to his own hand rather than
fall on its natural course. The Visitor in turn was
embarrassed not to be able to understand the Gray's
explanation of why what he had done was impossible.

*An image of Doth: a man carrying a lamp or pot of
fire, old and ragged, leaning on a staff.*

Learned Redhand's head was beginning to ache.
Perhaps he really hadn't done it at all... This Visitor
and the mystery of him grew quickly more exacerbating
than intriguing, like an answerless riddle. Even in the
bright winter light of the Harbor solarium, the Visitor
made a kind of darkness, as though the thick ambiguity
of the far past, leaking like a gas from the ancient
writings he pored over, clouded him.

"These images," the Visitor said, marking his place
with a careful finger before looking up, "they're all of
men or women. Why is that?"

"Well," Learned began, "the process of symbol-making..."

"I mean, for the names of weeks, it would seem one
at least would be, oh, a sheaf of wheat, a horse, a
cloud..."

"The ancient mind..."

"Is it possible that these names were once truly the
names of real men and women?"

"Well... what men and women?" The Gray idea of
the past, formulated like their simple, stern moral
fables out of long experience with the rule of men's
minds, was simply that before a certain time there were
no acts, men were too unformed or mindless to have
performed any that could be memorialized, and that
therefore, having left no monuments, the distant past
was utterly unknowable. Time began, the Grays said,
when men invented it, and left records to mark it by;
before then, it didn't exist. To attempt to probe that

darkness, especially through pre-Gray manuscripts that claimed to articulate beginnings by unintelligible "first images" and "mottoes" and "shadows of first things," was fruitless certainly, and probably heretical. "No," he went on, "aids to memory I think merely, however foolishly elaborate."

The Visitor looked at Learned's smooth, gracious face a moment, and returned to his reading.

An image of Barnol carries this motto: Spread sails to catch the Light of Suns.

An image of Athenol carries this motto: Leviathan.

"Leviathan," the Visitor said softly.

"An imaginary god or monster," said Learned. To the rational Gray mind the two were one.

Suddenly a servant stood in the solarium archway. The hall floors had been hushed with straw since Redhand had been brought home near dead; the servants moved like ghosts. "The Protector," he whispered, indicating the Visitor, "wishes to see you."

Leviathan . . .

The Visitor rose, nodded to Learned, went out behind the man and down twisting, straw-carpeted corridors.

Leviathan. It was as though the name had taken his hand in a darkness where he had thought himself alone. Taken his hand, and then slipped away. Gently, blindly he probed his darkness, seeking for its fearful touch again.

Redhand had grown older. He sat propped on pillows within a curtained bed; old, knowing servants made infusions and compresses, and the medicinal odor filled the high room. A large fire gave fierce heat, roaring steadily in the dim hush. Redhand's dark-circled eyes found the Visitor and guided him to the bed; he patted the rich coverlet and the Visitor sat.

"Do you have a name?" The Visitor could see in Redhand's face the unreasoning fear he had first seen in the forest; he could see too the broken body he had saved. Both were Redhand.

"They say—Visitor," he answered.

"That's . . ."

"It's sufficient."

"Fauconred has told me . . . incredible things. Which he apparently believes." His eyes hadn't left the Visitor. "I don't."

There was a gesture the Visitor had seen, had practiced privately when he had learned its vague but useful meaning. He made it now: a quick lift of shoulders and eyebrows, and return to passivity.

"You saved my life."

"I . . ."

"I want to . . . reward you, or . . . Is there anything you need?"

Everything. Could he understand that?

"There is a new King in the world. I have made him. Perhaps . . . it was wrong in me. Surely I have lost by it." *Take care*, his father had said. *Watch well*. "But there it is. I am made great now in the world, and . . ." He moved his knitting body carefully on the pillows. "Learned tells me you learn quickly."

"He tells me so too."

"Hm. Well. Learn, then. As long as you like. Anything you require . . . my house, servants are at your disposal." He tried to smile. "I will draw on your learning, if I may."

A silence, filled with the fire's voice. Already, it seemed to the Visitor, Redhand's thoughts were elsewhere. It was odd: he felt he had come a great distance, from somewhere no man had been, and carried, though he could not speak it, wisdom they could never here learn but from him. Yet they drifted off always into their own concerns . . . "You were at Redsdown," Redhand said. "You saw my lady there. She was well? Hospitable?" He looked away. "Did she . . . speak of me?"

"Often."

"She wrote me of you. This . . . airy talk."

The Visitor said nothing.

"I must regard you as a man."

"It's all I wish."

Redhand's eyes returned to him; it seemed they were again the eyes that had looked on him in horror in the Throat: alert with fear, yet dreaming.

"Who are you?" he asked.

Forgetful.

The Protectorate had built Forgetful as they had Old Watcher far away on the sunrise edge of the Drum, in the days after they had despaired of conquering the fierce, elusive tribes of the Outlands; built it to ensure that, if they could not conquer, at least they would not be conquered. The huge piles, strongly garrisoned, had made a semblance of diplomacy possible with the Outland chieftains; they had eventually accepted a king's lieutenant as their nominal ruler and only occasionally tried to murder him. Red Senlin had been one such; and before him, Black Harrah. The post at the moment remained unbestowed; but probably, Young Harrah thought, it will go to Younger Redhand for his infinite damned patience . . .

In Shensweek Young Harrah sat within the sweating, undressed stones of Forgetful, wrapped in a fur robe; completely safe, of course, but trapped in fact: it came to the same thing. With a lot of Outlanders for company, with spring coming but no help.

"Capitulate," he said.

"I don't see it," said the fat-cheeked captain he had taught to play War in Heaven—or at least move the pieces. The Outlander's thick fingers toyed with two sky-blue stones, moved them hesitantly amid the constellations pictured on the board. "Maybe you should capitulate."

"Move." Red Senlin's Son played at King in the City; the fat Queen, his father's whore, licked her wounds somewhere in the Outland bogs, whispering with the

braid-beards who adored her; and Redhand's mastiff
brother hung on here for life and would not be shaken.
It had been for a while amusing to watch them out
there, to make them endure a little privation before
they took their ugly and useless prize, this castle. The
game was no longer amusing. The Son played at King
in the City . . . there was the game. The Outlander
picked up the seven-stone, bit his lower lip, and set it
down in the same place. Young Harrah sighed.

"Now, now," said the Outlander. "Now, now." At
length he saw the trap and finessed gleefully. Young
Harrah tapped his foot, his mind elsewhere, and threw
a red stone across the sky without deliberating.

It was, of course, a struggle to the death. The Queen
believed Black Harrah slain by the Reds. For sure she
had slain Red Senlin the new King's father, and Old
Redhand too. There could be no forgiveness for that.
They must, he must, struggle with the King Red Senlin's
Son till Rizna called a halt. Yes. And he could think of
none else he would rather struggle with than the King's
blond limbs . . . With one long-toed foot he overturned
the War in Heaven in a clatter of stones. The Outlander
looked up. Young Harrah combed his blond hair with his
hand and said, "Surrender."

Along the wind-scoured Drumsedge, sterile land where
the broken mountains began a long slide toward the low
Outlands, it was winter still. The snow was a bitter
demon that filled the wagon ruts, made in mud and
frozen now, and blew out again like sand. Cloak-muffled
guards paced with pikes, horsemen grimly exercised
their mounts on the beaten ground. The wind snapped
the pennons on their staves, snatched the barks of the
camp dogs from their mouths—and carried from Forgetful's walls suddenly the war viol's surrender song, and
blew it around the camp with strange alteration.

Young Harrah led the morose Outlanders down the
steep gash in the rocks that was Forgetful's front way.
He rode with his head high, listening to•the distant

cheers of his victors. At a turning he could see Younger
Redhand and four or five others coming up toward him.
He dismounted and walked to where Younger awaited
him. He was amused to see that there had been time during the siege for Younger to grow a young man's mustache.
The cheering troops were stilled by a motion of Younger's
hand, and Young Harrah handed his sword up to him.

"Will I see the King?" he asked.

"Forgiveness," said the King. "Clemency."

The High City had been shaken out like a dusty rug
till it was clean of the gloom and shadows of Little
Black's reign. Great houses long shuttered were opened
and aired, streets were widened and new-paved with
bright stone. The City crafts, long in decline, suddenly
had to seek apprentices to satisfy the needs of the
great—for once more there were great in the City, their
carriages flew to the Citadel, they were received by the
King, they had audiences with Redhand; they were in
need of all things fashionable, these Downsmen were,
and their somnolent City houses were roused by a
parade of tradesmen knocking at their thick doors. The
cry of all stewards was for candles, good wax candles,
but there were none: there were rushlights and tallows,
torches and lamps and flambeaux—the candles had all
been taken to the Citadel to spangle the Ball.

"No seizures, no treason trials," said the King. "Not
now."

"If not now," said Learned Redhand, "then never.
You can't try old crimes years later."

"I meant," said the King, turning a moment from his
mirror, "no treason trials for these crimes. Later . . ."

The Ball is to be masked, a custom of ancient springs
revived. The King will appear as the Stag Taken in a
Grove—an image he discovered in an old Painted chamber, could not have conceived himself, there having
been no stags in the forests for uncounted years—and
as he was undressed and prepared he entertained Redhand

and his Gray brother, and Redhand's Secretary. Learned
would not go costumed, a Gray may not; but he carried
a long-nosed vizard. Redhand wore domino only, blood-
red. The King failed to understand why Redhand had to
have a secretary with him at a ball, but insisted that if
he must be here he must be masked. So the Secretary
consented to domino—even enjoyed its blank privacy.

"The Protectorate," Redhand said, "will praise you
for it."

"I know it."

"They are diminished in this war."

"I will rebuild them."

"Great landowners have been slain . . ."

"I will make new. Strictly"—bowing to Learned—"ac-
cording to the laws of inheritance." He raised his arms
for his dresser to remove his shirt. "Why do you
suppose, Protector," he said idly, "that we have been
able to do this thing?"

"What thing?"

"Pull down a king. Make a new king."

"Strength."

"Righteousness," Learned said graciously.

"Strength more nearly," said the King. "But private
strength. The strength of great men whose allegiance to
the old King lay only in an oath."

"Only?" said Learned.

The King smiled. "I mean that this that we have
done could be done again." He watched in the mirror
with dreamy interest as his dresser removed skirt and
leggings. "I would prevent that."

"By . . ."

"By making a new kind of Protectorate. One whose
loyalty lies here, in the Citadel. That looks for strength
less to some distant Downs and dependents than direct-
ly"—turning to them naked—"to the King's person."

Redhand, folded in his domino, was unreadable.

The King's dresser, with a whisper of fine fabric,
clothed the King in green, gorgeously pictured.

"The Grove," said the King. The room's candles played upon the stuff, making gold lights glitter in its leaves like noon sun. The King took from his dresser's hands a great head, contrived with golden horns that were as well a crown, and hung with ribbons.

"The Stag," he said. "The rose ribbons are its blood, these blue here its tears." He fitted the Stag's head to his own blond one, and was helped on with tall shoes that made dainty hooves beneath the Grove robe.

Despite himself, Redhand was moved by this splendor. Only—

"Where," he asked, "is the Hunter?"

There is a Rose with a Worm in its Breast, who laughs with a ghastly Suicide; there is a Cheese full of Holes who pretends fear of the Plate and Knife; there are two Houses Afire who are cool to one another; there is a Starry Night, there is a sheaf of wheat, a horse, a cloud.

There is a thing not man and not woman, made in a star: but he is disguised as Secretary to the Great Protector Redhand, and the Secretary is wrapped then in red domino like his master.

Where is the Hunter? He is all in green leather, belted and buckled, he has bow and ancient darts.

When the Stag sees him, he leaps to run, striding on his tiny hooves through the startled crowd. The music stumbles; the Chest of Treasure stops dancing with the Broken Jug, who turns to the Mountain; he jostles the Head without a Body so that his cup of drink is spilled.

Beneath a great circle of candles that overhang a dais, the Stag is brought to bay. He trembles; the candles as he trembles cast glitter through his moving Grove. The Hunter draws a dart and aims.

"What mummery is this?" Redhand asks, setting down his cup.

"Will he shoot the King?" asks his Secretary.

Redhand laughs shortly and pushes through the murmuring crowd of fantasies to where he can see.

"Strike now," says the Stag in a great voice. "I will no more fly thee; surely this day is made for thee, and thy hall shall rejoice in thy fortune."

The Hunter hesitates. "My arm refuses my command, my fingers rebel against my hand's wish."

"See," the Stag cries out, "thy spade has struck a red spring; the well is thine to make; make it quick."

The Secretary whispers in Redhand's ear: "The words. They are a song in the Thousand and Seven Songs."

"Yes?"

"Yes. It's a . . . love song."

"Why dost thou weep?" the Hunter asks, lowering his bow. "Have we not chased fair all the day long, and hast thou not eluded me time and again, when I thought all lost and might have departed, and is this now not well done, that I have brought thee by my strength to this?"

"It is well done."

"Weep not."

"I must."

"I cannot strike."

"Where are your black Hounds then, that have drawn so much red blood from me?"

" 'Black Hounds' is wrong," the Secretary whispers to Redhand. "There were no Hounds. In the song he does . . . strike."

"Watch," says Redhand. "I begin to understand this."

At the Hunter's signal, there leap forth seven black Hounds, who rush the Stag to worry him. From his Grove as the Stag cries out (or from the arras behind him) come forth seven red Wounds. The Starry Night beside Redhand cries out. The Hounds fall back then, covering their eyes.

"They are amazed," the Hunter cries. "They will do no further harm, seeing you in this distress."

"Command them."

"I cannot! My tongue rebels against my thought to say it!" Suddenly, as though in great agony, he rushes to the dais and falls before the Stag, making obeisance. "Noble, noble beast! Each wound you take is as a wound to me. Each Hound that savages you"—summoning them with his hand so they make obeisance too—"seems to make me bleed. Forgive me this and all outrages! I will do no murder on thee nor ever seek again to draw thy red blood!" He breaks across his knee his fragile play-bow. "And these mute"—indicating his cowering Hounds—"I ask in their names the forgiveness of the mute blood they have shed."

"Rise, brave Hunter!" cries the Stag joyfully. "Wear brown not green, for with these words my wounds begin to heal..." He makes a subtle cue, and the music strikes up; each of the Hounds embraces a Wound. "I do forgive you! You and all these brave, more than brave in this asking. Come!" He bends, takes up the Hunter; the music peals merrily. He draws off the Hunter's mask of green leather.

Young Harrah, flushed with his acting, turns smiling to the astonished company.

They are silent. The music trembles in a void.

Redhand, stepping forward, throwing back his domino to reveal himself, begins to applaud. His applause rings hollowly for a moment, a long moment, and then the Starry Night begins to clap; then the Cheese and the Suicide, the House Afire and the Chest of Treasure. The Stag, immensely pleased, draws Young Harrah and Redhand together to embrace. The fantasts push forward applauding to congratulate.

Redhand takes Young Harrah's arm. "Unfortunate," he says, "that the Queen who was so eager in this same chase is not here to be forgiven." Young Harrah looks at him, the smile wavering. "You found my brother well?"

"He found me, Protector."

"Is he in health? I ask only because his health is not good, and the winds of the Edge..."

"Protector," says Young Harrah with the faintest edge, "your brother came to me as conqueror, not acquaintance. I did not inquire after his welfare."

"Well. Well. Now if I read this show rightly, we are here both made brothers of the Stag. I would have you be that to me, neither conquered nor acquaintance."

He is granted a half-smile by the Hunter, who turns to take others' hands.

"These others," Redhand says to the Stag. "I think I know them. Will we see their faces?"

Dumbshow: each of the seven Hounds removes his hairy head, each of the Wounds puts back his red-ribboned cloak.

"As I thought," Redhand says to his Secretary. "Young Black defenders are the Hounds, younger sons of slain fathers, those who might have been marked for seizure. The innocent Wounds—is that what they were?—the King's brother Sennred, sons of intransigent fathers, small landowners, those . . ."

The last Hound has shown himself. A thick, brutish head, more houndlike than his mask. It is a face Redhand vaguely knows: a certain bastard son of Farin the Black.

The Stag has begun to speak again, of love, reconciliation, a new bright order of things. Redhand turns away, pushing aside the murmuring guests, and leaves the floor.

"Sweet, come to bed."

None sees but the eyeless Stag's head, thrown upon a chair.

"I will not be mocked." Young Harrah drinks off the last of a cup, naked by the curtained bed.

"No one mocks you." The King puts off the Grove robe, lets it fall with a rustle. "Come to bed."

"Redhand."

"Redhand," the King says. "Redhand is a man of mine. He will love you for my sake."

"He would be your master."

"I have no master."

The room is smoky with incense; the bed hangings
Harrah draws aside are fine as smoke. "None?"

"None other." He moves impatiently within the bed.
"Love. Master me." He reaches out and draws Harrah
down amid the clothes. "Master me. Master me . . ."

2

It was as if, that spring, all eyes and ears turned Inward
to the City on the Hub within its ring of mountains.

The King's appetite for shows, triumphs, displays
grew larger; unappeased by the ragtail pageant-carts
that on glum street corners gave shows everyone knew
by heart, he commissioned his own, drawn out of
ancient stories by eager young men, stories full of new
wit and unheard-of spectacle. Guildsmen of the City
put their tools to strange uses building the machinery
for abductions, enthronements, clockwork miracles—and
the cleverest of them were paid well, in bright coinage
the King had struck showing not a crude denomination
but his own profile—too lovely almost to spend.

He was, though, his own most striking show. With
his crowd of young Defenders, all handsome, all proud,
with a canopy over him and men-at-arms before him
with fantastical pikes and banners, he rode through the
City weekly, visiting the guildhalls and artisans' shops,
viewing construction of arches and the preparation of
plays, of *The Sword Called Precious Strength* or *The
Grievances Brought to King Ban;* always on his right
hand Young Harrah, on his left Redhand, Master of the
City, with his shadow Secretary all in red domino; and
behind, close behind, his brother Sennred.

The King's brother Sennred was as small and dark as

the King was tall and fair; some said another man than
Red Senlin must have been Sennred's father, that when
Senlin was King's Lieutenant in the Outlands, some
other . . . but none said it to his face.

Sennred's right shoulder was higher than his left, and
they called him stooped for it; but it was only constant
practice with the sword that made it so: practice that
had made him a match for any man living, though not,
he thought, therefore worthy of his brother's love.

The banner carried before Sennred in these pomps
was the Dog; he had chosen it himself; he had made
himself watchdog to his brother, and when the counsel-
ors departed, and the bodyguards slept, and the King
was drunk and went abroad looking for his lover at dead
of night, there was still one who watched, mute as a
hound.

Who watched now, half-hearing the banter between
Young Harrah and the King, and Redhand glum and
unfashionable beside them.

Redhand. Sennred had once mistrusted Redhand,
had thought that when danger came Redhand would
turn on the Senlin clan. Then their fathers had died
together at Forgetful, and Sennred had fought beside
Redhand at the Little Lake: and he had yielded up to
Redhand a share of his dark love. It hurt him now to
see his brother turn from Redhand; hurt him more to
see he turned to Young Harrah.

That Sennred longed to shed Young Harrah's blood,
wound him in secret places, none knew, for none asked
Sennred's opinions. It was as well.

They wound down Bellmaker's Street slowly, moving
through throngs of people eager to touch the King (few
had ever so much as looked up from their work to see
Little Black pass); eager too for the new coins he
dispensed.

It was as well. For Sennred knew where the King's
love lay, and he would die rather than harm it. But
Redhand . . . Now the tolling and tinkling drowned out

the laughter of the King with Young Harrah; Sennred saw them turn laughing to Redhand, who turned away. Sennred pushed forward, waving aside the pikemen, and took Redhand's arm in the strong grip of his sword hand.

"There is another joke," he said to Redhand beneath the bells' voices. "They ask at court who holds the King's scepter now." He stared up at Redhand unsmiling. "Do you understand? Who holds the King's scepter now."

Angry, red-faced, Redhand pulled himself from Sennred's grip and forced his way out of the procession, through the curious crowd, out and away down the Street of Goldsmiths, his Secretary close behind him.

A great yellow Wanderer came full that night and shone in the streets of the City, on closed carriages, on late carousers in rumpled costumery; calm, female, it stroked the narrow streets and high houses with pale light. It shone on two walkers, one in domino, turning their red to neutral dark.

Since being made King's Master of the City, Redhand had often walked away sleepless nights along its arching streets; had learned it like a footpad, knew its narrow places, its silences, its late taverns and late walkers—watermen and whores, watchmen and those they watched for, lovers alone together: found a comfort in it he never found in the silences of his Redsdown parks. No Master of the City knew the City as Redhand did; Black Harrah, when he went from the Citadel to his estates, went in a closed carriage.

They looked down, Redhand and his Secretary, onto the soundless lake from an ancient arched bridge.

If you kick me I will bite you to the bone.

In the row of shacks along the water's edge one light was lit. From that doorway a slim, tall figure came carrying a bundle, put it in a small boat and pushed off onto the lake, where the Wanderer's light trembled.

"The King," the Secretary began, "and Young Harrah . . ."

"They must know," Redhand growled. "They must
know I will kill him if I can."

That Wanderer had set; another, palely blue, had
risen when she reached the far margin of the lake. She
nudged her boat in among the small craft sleeping
there, and, stepping from deck to deck as though on
stepping stones, came out on the wharf. Someone
called out, and she answered in a waterman's singsong
call; the someone needed to know no more, and was
silent. She waited a long moment in the shadow of a
winch piling, listening for other sounds than the lake's;
heard none, and went quickly up the water-stairs to
where they joined the highway into the mountains.
There she did not approach the guardhouse for permission to enter the road, but, with a silence learned
elsewhere than on the water, dropped into the brushy
woods that ran along it.

The guardhouse torches that lit the road's wide mouth
were far behind when she again stopped for a long
moment, listening for other sounds than the forest's.
Again she heard none, pulled herself up by the tangle
of brush at the road's edge and stepped out onto the
smooth blue highway, elated, walking with long strides
at deep midnight.

Her name was Nyamé and the name of her name was
Nod. Her Gun's name was Suddenly. She carried Suddenly in a pouch of oiled goatskin at her side, the kind
watermen carry their belongings in, for she was a
waterman's daughter: that is, Nyamé was. Nod was
Just. Suddenly had said so.

Wet winds had bridged the days where Fain met
Shen, and then had turned warm and dry; now beneath
her feet the pavingstones were green with moss, and by
the roadside tiny star-shaped flowers had sprung up.
The hood of her no-color traveler's cloak, that covered
goatskins, Gun, and all, was thrown back, and the

nightwind tickled her shorn blond head; it seemed to speak a word in the budding forest, a word she could almost hear: *awake*, yet not that either. It bore her up; almost without knowing it, in answer to the hushing wind, she began to sing.

The tunes were tunes the Folk had always sung, so much alike that one slid into another at a change without her choosing. The words, though, were the Just's: mournful and hopeful, silly and sad. She sang of old, old things, of gods long asleep, of the Fifty-two, unborn, sky sailors; she sang, skipping a few steps, rhyming puns that mocked the King and all his lords, made them dance a foolish dance before they fell down dead, as fall they all must one by one: for she sang too of her Gun and its hunger. She sang of the Deep and its beings, of Leviathan curled around the pillar of the world, dreaming all things that were, old and memorious when even the Grays were young. She sang, tears starting in her eyes, of being young, and brave, and soon to die:

I lay on the hillside
I dreamed of Adar.
"King Red lies at Drumriven
But he'll rise up no more.
This one I call Shouter of Curses,
This is the flint, this the ball I will feed him
To spit in King Red's eye."

I woke on the hillside
The brothers and sisters were gathered.
"King Red lies at Drumriven
A stone ball in his forehead.
But the one called Shouter of Curses is broken
And Adar's flesh stills the hounds that mourn King
    Red."

Adar, the grass grows still on the hillside
The long, forgetful grass that covered us:
Why, why will you not come to where I lie waiting?

The paved highway soon gave way to dirt rutted with
spring rain, and the dirt often to a lane, marked only by
stern stone bridges the ancients had built to arch the
deepest ravines. These she kept count of, and at the
fifth, as the sun and a thin mist were rising together,
she stopped; she looked quickly behind her and then
went into the ravine beneath the bridge. A path, that
might have been made by rain but hadn't been, led
steadily downward, deep beneath the aged trees whose
tops filled up the ravine. As she went, what seemed
impassable from above became more and more an easy
glen in the gloom below. She ate bread and cheese as
she walked, listening to the birds awake; and before the
mist had entirely burned away, she stood before the
Door in the Forest.

Had there ever truly been one called Adar?

She knew of some who had named their names for
him. Yet for sure King Red had died in his sleep at a
great age, imprisoned in the Citadel.

Once, so long ago no one now knew his or the King's
name, one of the Just had killed a king.

And now, she thought, the kings kill each other. May
they, she prayed, go on doing so until the last of their
line stands alone, deserted, with his prize that crown,
alone before the Just; and may a Gun then speak
intimately with him; and the Folk be at last made free.

In her lifetime, in her youth? How many of the Just
had wondered that, since how long ago . . .

To any not allowed to pass through it, any not Just,
the Door in the Forest would not have seemed a door.
It was only a narrow way between the entangled roots
of two elder trees, with impassable deadfalls on either
side; yet she was careful to make all the proper signs to

the Door's guardians she could not see but knew were watching there.

Beyond the Door was much the same as before it; here too was dim glen and the birds awaking. Yet she felt she had left all her fears at that Door, and had come at last home. When the path at length came out of the grove and opened out into a wide meadow, she could see far down the whole length of the valley; beyond this meadow another meadow and another went on like pools of grass in the forest, down to where the stony sides of the valley seemed to close a farther Door. Then sheer mountains rose up; far, far away was a pale glitter: sunlight striking the white stones of Inviolable. She could see it, but it couldn't see her: a thrill of private pleasure.

Here, at the edge of the meadow, new moss spangled with flowers made a bed, and she lay gratefully, suddenly exhausted; the Gun in its pouch she laid beside her, and her pack under her head, and slept.

She woke because she felt a presence. She had forgotten where she was, or when she had come there, or what time of day it now was: but she knew someone was near, and watching. She sat up with a start, and seemed at the same time to coalesce here: late afternoon, beyond the Door, and a boy, Just, before her, smiling.

A mirror image of her almost, he had her blond short hair, her pale eyes, her long limbs, and she smiled his smile. His homespun was faded to a blue like his eyes—as though it were part of him, it was creased for good, like his hands, smooth and useful as his naked feet. Across his back, as long almost as he, hung a black figured Gun.

From a pouch he drew a handful of gray withering leaves. "I gathered these for you."

"How did you know I was here?"

He smiled. "I found you hours ago. Gathered these. I've been watching you sleep."

As he said it, she seemed to remember dreaming of him. "What is your name called?"

"My name is called Adar."

"My name is called Nod." Not her name, but what her name was called. Why did it seem to reveal her more to say it than to say her name?

Adar had found a flat stone and laid the gray leaves on it; with flint and steel he started the little pile smoldering. Hungrily Nod bent over it, beckoning the smoke into her face with her hands and breathing it in. Adar did the same when Nod moved away satisfied; they bent over it in turns till it was all pale ash. And sat then together, looking out over the valley.

Though woolly clouds rose over and crossed the valley, to them now it seemed that the valley turned beneath still clouds, sharp and clear as though painted for some vast pageant. So the wind too, which moved the clouds, seemed to be rather the valley's passage through still air: they at its center watched the world turn beneath the sky.

Then the turning valley entered new country: the clouds it moved under were denser, gray as lamb's wool, and the valley moved faster through cool, wet air that stirred their hair and opened their nostrils. The valley groaned in its quickened passage, ground rocks perhaps that sparked pale lightnings: then its forward edge passed through a curtain of rain, and the fat drops filled up the air, startling them and dispelling their dream. They moved close, back into the dense grove that was suddenly noisy with rain; found themselves tasting each other's rain-wet flesh.

His hunger surprised her; she herself felt cool, poised, as she liked to feel before doing a dangerous thing, though often didn't; she relished the feeling now, helping his helpless-eager hands undo her. She let him feast on her, let herself by degrees expand with heat out of her reserve until she must cry out: letting herself cry out felt like falling backwards when something soft is

sure to break the fall. Her cry stilled him, his hands
grew less sure; so she began to take him, moving the
smooth homespun from his smooth flesh.

Thunder beat on them. The grove grew wild and
dark with storm.

It had always fascinated her, blind, eager, so helpless
and vulnerable and then too imperious, not to be
denied. She felt once again poised, but now on some
higher peak, ready to leap yet delaying. He made some
motion toward her, it didn't matter, this one held her
with its blind eye: when she took it, it leapt in her hand
as though startled.

Around her as she woke the grove let drops fall from
leaf to shuddering leaf. Outside, the clouds were dark
rags against pale night sky where only the brightest
stars could be seen. Around the meadow sat many, in
dark groups of two or three, the long black of their
Guns sharp in the weird light. More came from the
forest and the valley below, noiselessly, calling out in
the voices of night things to announce themselves. Adar
was gone.

It was this she had come for.

At the meadow's center, a pavilion, a gesture toward
a pavilion—two slim stakes, a gauzy banner, a rug
thrown over the wet grass. On the rug Someone to
whom, singly, each in the meadow came. Nod waited,
watching, till she felt some invisible motion in the
whole of them that brought her to her feet, moved her
in her turn to the pavilion.

Slim, soft, white as Death, maned with white hair,
the Neither-nor perched upon the rug like an ungainly
bright bird. Laid out on the painted board before It
were the painted cards of an oblong deck.

The Neither-nor, neither man nor woman, arbiter of
the Just, keeper of the Fifty-nine Cards and of all
secrets. It—not-he-not-she—resolved in Its long, fragile body the contradictions that the rulers of this world

(and their Gray minions especially) would keep at war: ruler and ruled; good and evil; chance and certainty; man and woman.

Since the Just had been, such a one had guided them; since the first appeared, ages ago, to free men from tyranny. That first Neither-nor had appeared out of nowhere, pure emanation of the Deep or the heavens, bearing in one hand the Cards, in the other a Gun—sexless, without orifice or pendants; birthless, without omphalos; deathless, who had only Departed and left nothing behind.

This Neither-nor, successor to the first, holy body of Chalah, Two Hands of Truth, threw down Its paint pot and bit of mirror in disgust. In this light, Its eyes could not be made to look the same. . . . Its anger passed, dispersed by a motion of the Two Hands. Nod came close to sit before It; It turned Its fabulous head to look at her; within the softness of Its face Its eyes were still fierce and male somehow. For this Neither-nor was not clean of sex, not truly neither, but only both, vestigially. It had been taken, soon after birth, by the Just, raised up to be successor to the old Neither-nor when It would die. So this one would die, too: was only human, however odd. But there was this Providence, and always (the Just believed) had been: the Neither-nor was Just, most Just of them all; wise; chose well from the Cards whom the Guns would speak to; watched their secrets well, and would die to keep them secret. It was enough. The Neither-nor received their love, and gave them Its love freely, even as It dealt Death.

"Child." With a jingle of bracelets It reached out a Hand to stroke Nod's shorn head. "Many have told me of Black Harrah." Its fluid fingers turned and turned the Cards. "Do you know. I have a stone, a leaf, a bit of earth from the places where six of your brothers and sisters lie, six who drew Black Harrah from my cards?" Nod could say nothing. The Neither-nor regarded her, a tiny smile on Its mauve lips. "Do you come again then so soon to draw another?"

"What else could I do, Blessed?" It was not bragging; in the winey, wind-blown night, chill after rain, here before fate, Nod felt transparent; her words to the Neither-nor seemed so truthful as not to be hers at all. The Neither-nor lowered Its head, made a tiny motion, turned a first card. Nod began to speak, telling what her life had been, plainly; what she had seen; who of the great she had been near. Once the Neither-nor stopped her, said over what Nod had said: "In Redhand's train, dressed in red domino . . ."

"A naked face, his eyes not like men's eyes. In the battle with the Queen, it was he who saved Redhand when he fell . . ."

She watched as the Neither-nor turned down a card: it was an image of Finn, with a death's head and a fire lit in his belly. It had this motto: *Found by the lost*. "Strange," the Neither-nor whispered. "But no, not him . . . Go on. Is there Young Harrah in it?"

No, Nod thought. Not both father and son. Let the cards say not so . . . She went on slowly, watching the silent fall of the cards.

"They call themselves Brothers of the Stag." She swallowed. "They are both Red and Black, and say they have put aside their quarrel to all serve the King. Young Harrah is their chief . . ."

The Neither-nor turned down a card. "Not Young Harrah, then. Here is Chalah."

The deck the Neither-nor read from contained fifty-two cards, each a week, and seven trumps. These trumps were they whom the Grays called the Possessors, whom the Seven Strengths did endless war with in the world and in men's hearts. The Just knew otherwise, that there were but Seven and Seven alone, and contained the contradiction that for their own ends the Grays had turned into open war so long ago. At the turn of each trump, the Neither-nor named it; for it was these Seven who ruled Time, which is the Fifty-two.

Chalah, who is Love and its redemption, is also Lust and its baseness.

Dindred, who is Pride, Glory, thus Greatness in the world's eyes, is also blind Rage, thence treachery and ingloriousness.

Blem, who is Joy and good times, Fellowship and all its comforts, is too Drunkenness, Incontinence and all discomforts.

Dir, who is Wit, is the same Dir who is Foolishness.

Tintinnar is the magnanimity of Wealth, the care for money, thus meanness and Poverty.

Thrawn is Strength and Ability, exertion, exhaustion, and lastly Weakness and Sloth.

These six, when they fall upon a name, shelter the one named, or throw obstacles in the path of the Just were they to pursue him; thus Chalah, for a reason the Neither-nor could not tell, protected Young Harrah. Nod went on, her heart beginning to tap at her ribs.

"Redhand stays apart from them, though he wears the badge too. He gathers strength. His brother Learned is a dark Gray. His brother Younger holds the castle Forgetful. His father is slain, all his father's honors and lands are his. He is greater than the King..."

Lips pursed, the Neither-nor turned down the last trump.

Rizna is Death. Death and Life, who carries the sickle and the seedbag, and ever reaps what he continually sows.

"You are brave," It says in Its sweet, reedy voice.

"No."

"Implacable."

She cannot answer.

"Just."

"Yes."

"I think you are." It slides Rizna reversed toward Nod. "Are you afraid?"

"Yes." Till Death—his or hers—they have been wedded here.

Tears have suddenly begun to course down the Neither-nor's white cheeks. It is an ancient being; so many fates has It read, so many It has sent to death; weeps now because It can see nothing.

"Redhand," Nod says, trying to take him by the name. "Redhand."

The Arbiter Mariadn is dying.

The old, old grayest of all Grays lies propped on pillows within her chaste apartment. Its casement windows have been opened to the garden, though the doctors think it ill-advised, and a breeze lifts the edges of many papers on tables.

Her face is smooth, ashen, calm. Before sunset, before morning surely, her heart will stop. She knows it.

Through all this week they have come, the great Grays and the lesser, from every quarter, from the court, the law offices, the country seats, foregathering here like a summer storm. For a time she could feel their presence in Inviolable, in the chambers outside her still room; they have mostly faded now. Her world has grown very small; it includes the window, the bed, the servant ancienter even than herself, her dissolving body and its letting go—little else now.

The servant's face, a moon, orbits slowly toward her. *Has he come yet?* she thinks she asks. When the servant makes no reply, she says again, with pain this time, "Has he come yet?"

"He is just here."

She nods, satisfied. The world has grown very small, but she has remembered this one thing, a thing expressed in none of the wills and instruments she has already forgotten. She would have it over; does not wish it, an oath in an autumn garden, a thing still left to do, to intrude on her dissolution, a process that has broken open all her ancient locked chests, torn down her interior walls, let past light in to shine on present darkness: the light of a farm on the Downs, in the spring, in seedtime, warming young limbs and brown earth . . .

He has been there some time when she again opens her eyes.

"Learned."

"Arbiter."

"They will not deny me . . ." She stops, her lips quivering. She must not ramble. There must be strength for this. There is: she draws on it, and the world grows smaller. She calls her servant. "Call them now. You know the ones. Those only."

She takes his warm hand in her cold. "Learned, lean close . . . Learned, my successor will be named by the Councils. Hush, hush . . ." He had begun some comforting words. There is no time for that; her time spills as from a broken clock. "Help me now. For our Order's sake. You must; you have no choice, no reason to deny me that can stand. Lift me up. They've come."

A cloud of smoke at the bed's end coalesces into faces, forms. Many she has known since they were boys and girls; it seems they have changed not at all. She must be firm with them. "I would have Redhand succeed me." She cannot tell if they are looking at her, at Redhand, at each other. It is too long ago to remember which is which, who would accede, who would be swayed by which other. It doesn't matter. "There is no time or strength left me to argue it. Take him at my word or do not. But let not one of you desire my place. Shun it. I place on Redhand only labor and suffering. Remember that. If you will not have him whom I name, let whomever you name have your pity and your love."

All done; and the last of her strength leaks away. She finds it hard to listen to the words spoken to her, Arbiter, Arbiter; she has forgotten why this man should not be excluded from her world like all else, except that his hand is warm and his voice pleasant though senseless.

Done. Sunset has come suddenly, the room is dark.

Her little world with a grateful sigh shuts up small,
smaller than a fist; it draws to a fine point and is gone.

And yet, and yet—strange: even when she is cool on
the white-clothed bed, still the sunlight enters soundlessly
in at the casements, the wind still lifts the corners of
many papers on tables. In the garden trees still drop
blossoms on the paths that go their ways; Learned
Redhand at the casement can see them, and can feel on
his face the hot, startling tears, the first he has shed
since he put on Gray.

3

To my best-loved Caredd, at Redsdown:
He who bears this is known to you, and can tell you much
that is too long for this.

You must know that the Arbiter Mariadn is dead. It was
her wish, and the Grays in Council acceded to it, that my
brother Learned be successor to her. This is great news
and cause for celebration—no other in our family has risen
so high in this. The ceremonies & all else attendant on this
have been secret in part & I have heard of them only
through Learned's hints, but it is all very solemn and
grand.

So this must be celebrated! You write me that the lambs
are fallen & the rabbits everywhere bold; well, then, there
will be a feast at Redsdown, such as this soft age has not
seen, that your father's father might have been satisfied to
sit at. I leave it to your good judgment, & know that all
you do will honor us.

If it cannot be Rokesweek Eve, write quickly and give it
to Ham to carry. I will say Rokesweek Eve if I hear
nothing.

My duty etc. to our mother there, and kiss my girl for
me. I mean to set out this week eve.

By he who bears it, at the Harbor, Devonsweek.

Beneath his signature, in his own tiny, long-tailed hand:

Caredd, there are those here who say they are not enemies to me and whom I do not fear but mistrust. They are partly the King's creations; they are little men of no consequence, for all they wear the King's badges and style themselves Brothers of the Stag. If such a feast as I mean could show such ones what it is to be Protector of men and lands, such would not be from my purpose. I know you know my mind; you ever have. R.

She folded the crackling paper and smiled at its bearer. "Welcome to Redsdown," she said. "Welcome back."

"It's good to be back." This the Secretary knew to be the right response, but in fact it seemed to him odd in the extreme to have returned here: it was the first place on his journey he had returned to, and he half-expected that from here he would return to the horse-gathering, the Endwives' cottage, the egg... "And good to see you." It was: her autumn-brown eyes and careful hands, her auburn hair stirred in him the devotion he had felt that autumn. He watched her, feeling himself suddenly to be One, as he had felt the King and Redhand to be One... no. Not wholly like.

She took his arm and led him up through the garden he had found her in, the garden mad with spring and sun, toward the low dark of the hall. "You are Secretary to my husband now."

"Yes."

"No longer Possessed, or some creature?"

He couldn't answer.

"You'll keep your secret, then."

"I don't know how to tell it."

"You must have many new ones now. City secrets, policy..." She summoned up vague and dangerous knowledge with her hand.

"I am a Secretary," he answered. "It's not... what

was intended, I don't think. If I could, I would forget—
all else. It's sufficient."

"Learned . . ."

"Taught me much. To read. To learn old knowledge."
Like a shudder, he felt it come and pass again: *Leviathan*. "Yet never who or what I am. I intend now to
serve Redhand."

She looked at him; his blank face still showed no
trace of a man behind it, the eyes were still pools of
unknowable dark.

"And serve you too," he said. "If I am allowed."

She smiled. "You have grown gracious in the City.
Yes. Serve me. Tell me of these Brothers of the Stag
and if there is danger to Redhand. Help me in this
feast." Her smile faded. "Watch Redhand. You saved
him in battle. You have strengths that frighten me.
Watch Redhand, ever."

He would. If it were not the Task he had been made
to do, not the Direction he had been made to take, it
came from her. It would do.

Late, late, Redhand came to her. Below, the guests
who had arrived with him at sunset went on with their
play, though now it was near sun again. All night since
his arrival, he had been with her only as master of
Redsdown with its mistress; she had watched him
shepherding his City friends and these Brothers of the
Stag from drink to supper to drink again with a set and
icy smile she had not known before. She had watched
him, and Learned, for whom after all tomorrow's feast
was made, left out of jokes or made the butt of them—
so it seemed to her, though they both smiled, and
Redhand poured cup after cup of drink, not drinking
himself, as though he were afraid of Blem's indiscretion. . .

And then late, late, after she had been driven to bed
by the malice and queerness she felt in the King and
his young men, Young Harrah especially, Redhand came
to her.

Plunged himself within her warm coverlets, silent, hasty, so needful it was hard for her to keep up with him, yet so fierce that he carried her along as in a storm.

Later, a chill summer rain began.

It seemed to Redhand that it always rained when he came to Redsdown. Always. Passion spent, he felt that fact weigh on him with an awful injustice, filling him with black self-pity, till he must get up from the bed and pull on his shirt, light a light and go to the gray window to watch it fall.

In a while, awakened by his absence, she called to him in a small voice.

"It was the rain," he said.

She stirred within the bedclothes. "What do they intend?"

"They?"

"Below. The King."

He said nothing, not knowing himself.

"Harm? To us?"

"And if they did?"

Rain fell with a constant sound. The darkness spoke to him again: "The King," she said. "Young Harrah is . . . They have some plan."

"They come at my invitation. To a feast. They have no plan." It put him in mind of them, hinting smugly at what they did not dare execute, at revenge they were too weak to take, power they could not seize. Not from Redhand. His head drew down to his wide shoulders, bull-like, as he thought of them. "Let him suck the King. Let them make their jokes, who holds the King's scepter. They are insects at a candle flame . . ."

She knew then, as she held still to hear his gritty voice, that she had been right, that the King intended if not her husband's death then his ruin; and that Redhand did not know it.

The feast day brightened; the rain began to blow away toward the City.

"Shall we go in, then?"

Fires had been lit in the apartments and anterooms of Redsdown, despite the new summer; the old house's chill was not to be banished by a few weeks' sun. Learned Redhand stood before one, his hand with its dark agate ring on the carved mantel. In his other hand he toyed with a bit of flame-red ribbon.

"He comes," Fauconred said, "to a feast, with an armed guard larger than his host's household."

"A king's prerogative," Redhand said.

"Do you suppose," Learned said, "he has come to steal our jewels? Ravish our pages?"

Fauconred ran his fingers through his burr of gray hair. "I do not suppose, Learned." He turned to Redhand. "If I may, I will take my feast with the guard."

Redhand shrugged. "Now let us go in. Caredd..." He took her arm.

Learned turned from the fire, discarding into it the bit of ribbon, which was consumed before it met the flame, so fine a stuff it was.

Wide doors were thrown open, and they entered the hall, and all assembled rose with a murmur for the grayest of all Grays.

The last juggler dropped his last ball and was not invited to pick it up again. The musicians, prettily arranged around the entrance arch on a scaffolding or trellis of beams, flower- and banner-decked, fell silent; the musicmaster glanced at the steward, who glanced at Redhand, but received no cue.

There was the King left, and Young Harrah at his left side, and a few of the Brothers of the Stag. There was Redhand on the King's right side; there were some few others at the great tables piled high with ravished roasts

and pastries; some of them were asleep, face down on
the wine- and grease-stained tablecloths.

"Splendid," the King said. "So . . . antique."

Alone at one long table from which the Arbiter and
Caredd and the rest of Redhand's house had departed,
the Secretary to Redhand sat, peeling a fruit he did not
intend to eat.

"More of this?" Redhand asked, motioning a cup-
bearer. The King motioned him away.

Also sitting alone, the King's brother Sennred watched
the high table, keeping one hand on his sword. (Weapons, the feast-steward had said, were not allowed within
the banquet hall. Sennred had not replied, and the
steward had not repeated himself. Sennred's sword
slept with him. For sure it would feast with him.)

"This," said the King, "is a man's place. Here, on
land that is his, with his dependents around him. A
good farmer, a good neighbor." Young Harrah giggled.
"Your father and his must have sat here . . ."

"The land is mine by marriage," Redhand growled.

"Oh. I remember. The Red madwoman."

Redhand said nothing.

"I wonder," the King said, "what it is you find in the
City one half so precious as this you leave behind."

Redhand felt a sudden chill of premonition. All this
was another of their jokes, it had a cruel point to cut
him with he hadn't seen yet. He saw, though, that
Young Harrah had stopped toying with the remnants of
his feast.

"My duty," he said carefully, "requires me in the
City." The King was not looking at him. "I have the
City's gem, given me by your father."

The King reached out and with his long, careless
fingers lifted the heavy jewel that hung from Redhand's
chain. "Will you give it to me, then?" He asked it coyly,
teasingly, as one would a token from a lover.

"It is not mine to give."

"Is it, then," the King asked, "mine to give?"

"It is."

"And mine to take? It seems to me," he said, not waiting for reply, "that one with so many dependents, lands, a wife and daughter, might find this stone a heavy weight to bear."

Seeing at last what they intended, a weird calm subsumed Redhand's fears; he felt suddenly no further obligation to fence with them. Only let them not mock him further. "You've come for this."

"We will not leave without it." Young Harrah's voice was a light, melodic one; its tone never varied, no matter what he said with it. "I have seen enough of country pleasures for one year; the sooner gone the better."

"You see," the King said, "perhaps someone without these other responsibilities, someone..."

"Attached only to the King," Young Harrah said, smiling. "Someone..."

"Stop this." Redhand stood, tore the jewel from the chain and flung it down along the table. "I bought it with my father's blood. Can you return me that price?" He kicked back his chair the better to see Young Harrah where he sat; the chair's fall resounded in the high hall.

"You," he said. "Can you?"

Young Harrah regarded him. "Return you your father's death? I wish I could. It's not pleasant to remember."

"Not—pleasant." There was a sudden mad edge in Redhand's voice that made his Secretary stand.

"Your father," Harrah said coolly, "did not die well."

From the table Redhand snatched up a long bone-handled carving knife; the King stood to block his way, and Redhand threw him aside, reached Harrah and pulled him to his feet; slapped Harrah's face once, again.

Sennred was up, sword drawn. The King took Redhand's shoulder, Redhand pulled away and threw over the long table before them, dragged Harrah through the wreckage of dishes and cups to the center of the floor.

"Did not die well! Did—not—die well!" Redhand bellowed.

The Brothers of the Stag rushed forward shouting, and the King too, crying out, "Sennred!"

Redhand from a table took up another knife and thrust it into Young Harrah's hands. "Now fight me! Fight me, *woman!*" Again he slapped Young Harrah, and blood sprang from Harrah's nose.

Sennred reached them first, and turned to face the King and his Brothers, the quick sword against them. "Stand aside," he said quietly. "It is not your quarrel. Stand all aside." And they must.

Harrah held the knife before him, a quarry's fear in his eyes, and backed away, stumbling on spilled cups and rubbish; Redhand, heedless, moved on him, slashing with the unwieldy weapon, shouting at Harrah to fight. For a moment, desperate, Harrah stood, resisted; Redhand took a cut on the cheek, and at the same moment drove his blade deeply into Harrah's neck.

Harrah screamed, fell; his blood leapt, spattering Redhand. He twisted once, tried to rise, plucking at the blade in his throat; and then lay still, eyes wide.

There was a moment when no one moved, no one spoke.

Then someone struck Sennred from behind as he looked down, stunned, at Young Harrah; he fell sprawling across the floor, and the guests made for their host.

"Redhand!" The Secretary stood beneath the scaffolding at the archway. "Here!" He threw his arms around one of the thick beams that supported the structure and began pulling. It groaned, bolts popped, the musicians leapt and scrambled. Redhand ran through, with Farin's bastard son close behind. The Secretary strained, crying out with effort; the scaffolding swayed, splintered and collapsed before the archway, blocking pursuit.

Down the narrow corridors of Redsdown, doors

slammed around Redhand, running feet pursued him, more doors opened and shut behind him. He didn't turn to look; he followed the fleet shape of his Secretary where it led, till at the top of a stair he stopped, gasping. Running feet came on behind, he could not tell how close. The Secretary ran down and flung open the door at the bottom of the stair, and late afternoon light poured through it. "Here."

There were horses, saddled, waiting in the kitchen court beyond the door. For a moment Redhand stood, unable to run, from his home, from his act.

"They are in the Long Hall of the old wing," the Secretary said in his passionless voice. "The servants will not hold them long."

"No."

"Do you know a place to run?"

"Yes."

Still he stood; the Secretary at last came to him, took him like a child, pushed him down and out the door and away.

There was a twilight gloom in the stables. Farin's son stumbled, cursing, calling for grooms, a light, his horse.

A lantern flickered into life at the dark back of the stables.

"Groom! Bring that light here! Have they come here?"

"They?"

"Your master. That other. Who is it there? Can you get me my horse? Your master, boy, has done a murder and fled."

The lantern moved forward. "Who are you?"

Farin touched his sword. "A King's man. Farin's son. Stand where I can see you . . . Your master has slain a man and run, I think toward the Drumskin. Will you get my horse and help me, or . . ."

"Yes." The lantern brightened, was hung on a peg. A person, slim in a cloak of no color, stood in its yellow

light. "Let me ride with you. I . . . He came here, he
did come here, and I saw the way he went."

"Quick, then."

They worked fast, saddling Farin's black and a nag
the other found. From the castle above them they
heard shouts, cries, alarms. Redhand's household struggled with the King's guard.

"The lantern," Farin's son said, reaching for it.

"Leave it," said the other. "He will see it better than
we will see him by it."

In the stableyard some of the King's men fought with
Redhand's redjackets, vying for the horses who kicked
and showed teeth, maddened with excitement and the
smell of blood. Some redjackets moved to stop Farin's
son; he slashed at them, spurring his horse cruelly, and
forced a way to the stablegate leading Outward. From
there, they could see a troop of men, torches lit, riding
Outward in another direction: King's horsemen. "There,"
said Farin's son. "We'll join them."

"No. They're taking the wrong way. It was this way
he ran."

"But . . ."

"This way."

The nag began to canter, then broke into a swaying
gallop; the cloak's hood was blown back, revealing
short-cropped blond hair. Farin, looking after the others, stood indecisive.

"Come on, then! Would you have him?"

Farin turned his horse and caught up.

"Who was it murdered?"

"Young Harrah. There was not a finer, a sweeter
gentleman . . ."

In the growing darkness he could not see her smile.

For a week she had concealed herself at Redsdown,
in the woods at first, then on the grounds, finally within
the house itself, stealing food, hiding, losing herself in
the vast compound, not knowing even if Redhand were
there. She had seen him come then with the King and

the others, seen the feast prepared. It had ended thus. He was alone out there somewhere; alone, unarmed it might be.

"Stop," Farin's bastard said. "We go a quickwing chase here."

She had not thought this one would be fool enough to follow her so far.

A soft and windy night had come full. They stood on a knoll that overlooked grasslands, Redhand's grasslands that led Outward toward the Drum. They lay vast and featureless, whispering vague nothings made of grass and wind and new insects.

"Where are the others?" Farin said, standing in his stirrups. "I can't see their lights."

"No." She would need a better horse than this nag she rode; she would need other weapons, for silent work might need to be done. She must be quick; she must be the first to find Redhand.

"By now some of his people will have found him."

"Yes?"

"If we come upon them, they'll make a stand."

"Yes."

"We'll turn back then," Farin said.

She dismounted.

"Are you mad? We're alone here." She heard the jingle of his harness as he turned his horse, indecisive. "Will you search on foot? I'll return."

"Dismount, Farin."

"Stay, then!" she heard him shout at her turned back. "Join him, if that was your plan! Or have you led me away from him, knowingly?"

"Come, Farin. Dismount." Still her back was to him.

"You . . ." She heard him draw a sword, heard the horse turn on her. He meant to cut her down.

She turned. Suddenly.

It would have been easier if he had dismounted. She had but one chance, and must not hurt the horse. . . .

*   *   *

Night wind sent long shivers of light through the sea
of grass. The land seemed flat, but everywhere was
pocked with depressions, bowls, ditches. A man could
be sought in them for days; there were narrow, deep
places where two men and their horses could hide, and
look out, and see pursuers a long way off.

Far off, a sharp sound broke the night, echoed, was
gone. Redhand and his Secretary looked out, could see
nothing but starlight moving through the grass. No
further sound came to their hiding-place but the blowing of their spent horses. There was no pursuit.

Redhand knew many such places in the wide angle of
grass and Drumskin that was in his Protection; had to
know them, because the Just did, and from them at any
time outlaws might attack.

Outlaws. Murderers of the Protectorate, hidden in
holes.

He laughed, rolled on his back. Somehow Redhand felt
cleansed, free. Young Harrah lay at Redsdown: of all the
murder he had done, and it was much, he knew that that
one face at least would not return to look at him in dreams.

Above him the floor of heaven was strewn with
changeless stars. The Wanderers, gracious, benevolent,
made procession through them.

"You were born there," Redhand said to his Secretary.
It was a night to entertain such thoughts.

"Not born," the Secretary said. "Made."

"In a star?"

"No. In an . . . engine, set in heaven, set to circle like
the Wanderers. I think."

Redhand pillowed his head on his hands. On so clear
a night the stars seemed to proceed, if you stared at
them, ever so slowly closer. Yet never came near.

"What did it look like from there? Could you see the
City?"

"No." The Secretary turned from his watching to look upward with Redhand. "There were no windows, or I was blind, I forget..." Then the stars seemed to make a sudden, harmonious sound together, loud, yet far distant... He sat bolt upright.

"What is it? Do you hear pursuit?"

"No."

"Then what..."

"I did see it. I remembered, suddenly. Once. Many times, maybe, but it seems once. I saw it."

"And?"

So clear it was to him suddenly, as though it were his original thought, the ground of his being: "The world," he said, "is founded on a pillar, which is founded on the Deep."

"Yes," Redhand said. "So it is."

The Secretary watched the precious memory unfold within him; it seemed to make a sound, harmonious, loud yet far distant...

A chaos of dull darkness, unrelieved except by storms of brightness within it. Then a sense of thinning toward the top of view, and clarity. And then a few stars rose from the darkness, sparkling on a clear black of infinite dark sky.

"You arose from the Deep at morning," Redhand said.

Then there came far off a light, brighter than any star, rising up out of the dark and chaos, which seemed now to flow beneath him.

"Yes," Redhand said. "The sun, rising too out of the Deep."

The sun. It moved, rose up from the Deep blinding bright, cast lights down to the Deep below him. "Yes," Redhand said.

And there came the world. Merely a bright line at first, on the darkness of the horizon where the Deep met the black sky; then widening to an ellipse. The world, flat and round and glittering, like a coin flung on the face of the Deep. It came closer, or he grew closer to it—the sun crossing above it cast changing light upon it, and he watched it change, like a jewel, blue to white to green to veined and shadowed like marble. Only it, in all the Deep that surrounded it, all the infinity of dense darkness, only it glowed: a circle of Something in a sea of nothing.

And when he drew close enough he could see that the disc of the world rested on a fat stalk which held it up out of the nothingness, a pillar which for an instant he could see went down, down, endlessly down into the Deep, how far . . . but then the world was full beneath him, cloudy, milky green and blue, like a dish the arm and hand of an infinite Servant held up.

"Yes," Redhand said. "Just so."

The stars went by above, went their incomprehensible ways.

"Only," Redhand said, "you saw nothing of the Deep's beings."

"Beings?"

"Beneath the world. Oh, one's tail they say, the Just say, reaches around the pillar that holds up the world, and so he clings on, like ivy."

"I saw no such one."

"His name," Redhand said, "is Leviathan." His horse made a sound, and opened its nostrils to the night wind. Redhand turned to look across the Downs.

And how, the Secretary thought, am I to come to him then, beneath the world? And why has he summoned me?

"Riders," Redhand whispered.

They were a smudge only against the sky that lightened toward dawn; it could not be seen how many of them there were, but they moved slowly, searching; now two or three separated, went off, returned. Always they grew closer.

Redhand's horse stamped, jingling its trappings. They watched, motionless, ready to ride and flee, hopeless though that seemed. One rider, nearer to them than the rest, stopped, facing them. For a long moment he stood; then they could see his heels kick, and the horse ambled toward them. Stopped. And then faster, more deliberately, came for them.

Suddenly the Secretary was on his feet, running toward the rider, his domino picked up by wind, red as a beacon. The rider pushed into a canter.

"Stop!" Redhand cried.

"Fauconred!" the Secretary called.

"Redhand!" called Fauconred. He dismounted at a run and barreled into the Secretary, then came sliding hallooing down the slope of Redhand's hiding-place.

"Fauconred!"

"We've found you first, then! I think the King's men have given up. Are you unhurt?"

"The others . . ." They were gathering now, and he could see the red leathers of Fauconred's men, and the men on farm horses with rakes, the boys with scythes, the kitchen folk with cutlery. At Fauconred's ordering, they arranged themselves into a rude troop.

"Caredd . . ." Redhand said.

"They thought to take some action," Fauconred said.

"They dared not," one from the House said. "Not with the Arbiter there."

"She is in his protection."

"The King rages mad with this," said another.

"There are many of our people slain," Fauconred said. "The King's men hold the house and grounds. He'll be following, with an army. Already men have gone to raise his friends near here."

Redhand looked far away down the dawn, but he could see nothing of his home; only some few stragglers hurrying across the Downs to join them.

"Now," Fauconred said.

"Now." Redhand mounted. "Outward."

"Outward?"

"To Forgetful."

They followed him, his outlaw army; soldiers, cooks, farmboys.

And one who just then joined them, a boyish figure in a cloak of no color, riding a fine black horse.

4

There was a single window in the room where they had prisoned Caredd the Protector Redhand's wife and Sennred the King's brother. It was a blue hole pierced in the sheer curtain wall. The bricks of the wall were roughly masoned and a skillful man might crawl down, with a rope, a rope made of bedclothes... Sennred leaned far out and looked down, felt a weird fear grip his knees and pull him back. He hated high places, and hated his fear of them.

Below, in the dawn light of the courtyard of Redsdown, a knot of frightened servants was herded from the house by soldiers. Faintly he could hear pleas, orders. He turned from the window.

Caredd had ceased weeping.

She sat on the bed, eyes on the floor, hands resting in her lap.

"Lady," he said.

"Have they brought him back?" she asked, tonelessly.

"No," he said. "No, they have not."

He did not like to impose by sitting with her on the bed; he felt too implicated in her grief. So he had stood much of the night, trying in a helpless way to help, attempting lame answers to her unanswerable questions. Almost, at times, for her sake, he wished he had prevented what had happened in the banquet hall.

"Will they burn the house?" she asked.

"Never," he said, with almost too great conviction. "Never while the Arbiter is in it."

"And if he leaves?"

"He will not. Not till your safety is promised him."

They were silent awhile. The blue window brightened imperceptibly.

"What will they do to you?" she asked.

"I am the King's brother. Will you sleep, lady? No harm will come to you."

She had hardly looked at him, hadn't spoken except to question him; he could not tell if she hated him. For Young Harrah he had spared no thoughts. For himself he cared little. The thought that Redhand's lady suffered, because of him . . . her quiet weeping, nightlong, had been as knives to him.

"I think," she said quietly, "you must have done as you did . . . partly, at least . . . for his sake."

"I did," he said earnestly. "I did as I thought he wished me to, then." Was it so? "Perhaps I did wrong."

She looked up at him where he stood by the window. "I hope they will not harm you."

Perhaps the night's exhaustion, he didn't know, but suddenly he felt a rush of hot tears to his own eyes. He turned again to the window.

A troop of King's men were riding slowly up the road from the Downs. One man held the reins of a horse who plodded on, head down; over its back was flung a burden . . . "No!" he cried out, and then bit his lip in regret. But she had heard, and ran to the window beside him.

"They have brought him home," she whispered.

"Brought someone home."

"He was unarmed. There was no way he could have . . ."

"Lady, he was resourceful. And brave."

"*Was*. Oh, gods . . ."

"Is that his horse?"

"His? No, not any I know . . ."

"Where is his Secretary? Fled?"

"He would not have."

"He is not there."

She had taken Sennred's hand, perhaps not knowing it; gripped it tight. "They must let me see him!"

"They..."

"No! I will not! I couldn't..."

The troop entered the courtyard. What was now clearly a body swayed will-less on the nag's back. Caredd stared wide-eyed, mouth down-drawn. A boot dropped from one lifeless foot, a green and cuffed boot, a fashionable tasseled boot. Caredd cried out: "That isn't his!"

"Not his boot?"

She laughed, or sobbed. "Never. Never would he wear such a thing."

Sennred leaned far out the window, calling and gesticulating. "Who is it? Who is the dead man?"

A soldier looked up. "It is Farin's bastard son."

"Who?" Caredd asked.

"Farin's bastard," Sennred exulted.

"Shot with a Gun," the soldier called.

"A Gun! Where is Redhand?"

"Fled. Fled Outward with his people."

"Fauconred!" Caredd said. She began to slump forward. Sennred caught her around the waist and helped her to the bed.

"A Gun," he marveled. "The lout! Strikes out to find a murderer, and finds one. Of all nights in the year, flushes out such game! The idiot! I should have realized it from the first! He had a habit of drooling; he is well out of his miserable life... and tripping on his boots..."

"His green boots," Caredd said. "With the ridiculous cuffs."

"And tassels."

She laughed. She laughed with relief, with amazement, with grief, a long and rich and lovely laugh, without any edge of hysteria or exhaustion; her whole

body laughed, and her laughter poured over Sennred
like cool water.

The bar on their door slid back with a grating sound.

There was the Arbiter, and ten or twelve guards, and
two of the King's young favorites.

"Sennred," the Arbiter said. "They will take you to
the City."

"I will speak to the King."

"The King will not see you," said one of the young
Defenders.

"I will go nowhere without a word with the King."

"Sennred," Learned said, "I have taken a liberty. I
have promised them your good conduct in exchange for
the Lady Caredd's safety."

"And the house's safety," Sennred said. It had been
mostly what she talked of through the night.

"He will guarantee nothing beyond..."

"Listen to me," Sennred said to the King's men.
"Listen to me and tell the King. I am his heir. He will
have no other. If ever I am King and I find that any part
of this house, or any hair of this lady's head has been
harmed, I will spend my life and my crown and all its
powers to avenge it. Avenge it most terribly."

He looked once at Caredd, sitting shyly on the bed;
he heard an echo of her laughter.

"And now. We will go to the City."

It was Rennsweek of the vine flowers, strange brief
instant when all the world was summer, even the dun
country far Outward.

The broken rock walls of the Edge were bearded
with yellow-green; the ravines and crevasses, just for
this one moment, ran with water; tiny sun-colored
flowers nodded in the dry winds that would soon desic-
cate them. The few who lived this far Outward, solitary
people, gem hunters, ore smelters, people dun-colored
as the earth, smiled their one smile of the year this
week, it seemed.

The watch-castle Forgetful seemed to grow out of the dull earth, made as it was of the same stone, undressed, undecorated, rectangular indeed, but hardly more so than the split and shattered cliffs of the Edge it guarded. It had few windows, fewer doors; blind and mute. Only now, in this week, the endless scrollwork of vines which lashed Forgetful to the earth flowered bright orange briefly, so orange that anciently the flower's and the color's name were one word; and bees were drawn up from the Outland valleys to feed on the nectar that dripped from the fat blossoms as from mouths. And Forgetful in this one week seemed rightly named: Forgetful old tyrant with vine leaves in his hair, drunk on honey wine and Forgetful of a life of sin.

A tent and cave village squatted as the fortress's feet, serving the soldiers with all that soldiers have always been served with; a few of its low buildings, in parody of their master, were covered too with vine flowers. Two soldiers, on this day in Rennsweek, climbed up the stone way that led back to Forgetful from the village.

"Is he as bad, then?" the ostler asked.

"Worse than he was," the quartermaster said.

"Didn't the Endwife say spring would bring him round, and . . ."

"She said it was a melancholy."

"A soldier's malady."

"And if it weren't that, would she know?"

They paused for breath. The perfume of the vine flowers was thick. Forgetful motioned to them, almost gaily, with its fingers of vine leaves.

"He has ordered," the quartermaster said, "more stone on the . . . in the courtyard. And belts and spikes."

"To hold down the stones," the ostler said.

"Hasn't slept these three days."

"Dreams while he's awake, then."

The quartermaster shuddered. "I wouldn't have his dreams," he said. "Not for the wealth of Tintinnar."

Far above their heads, the war viols called alarm

from the battlements. The two scrambled up the rock walls to where they could see. Inward, Inward, the song called, and they looked Inward.

It could be no army; it had no wagons, no advance guard, no banners. It trailed out over the boulder-strewn plain in twos and threes; yet the ones in front wore red, and now as they looked a small detachment broke off and rode hard for Forgetful, unfurling as they rode a banner with a red open palm on it.

"Redhand."

"Come to pay his brother a visit."

"What are those weapons? A hoe?"

"A rake. Perhaps . . ."

"What?" the quartermaster said.

The ostler slid down from the rock. "Perhaps he's gone mad too. It should be a merry meeting."

In Forgetful's courtyard goats bleated, cookfires showed pale in the sun, curious soldiers lounged at doorways and looked down from parapets at the Army and House-hold of the Great Protector Redhand.

In Forgetful's courtyard, in the midst of this, there was a pile of stones half as high as a man. Over and through some of the stones ran leather straps and straw ropes, which were tied tight to stakes. The thing seemed weirdly purposeful, devised by a logic alien to the rest of the courtyard, the cooks, the goats, the soldiers, yet the center of all, like the altar of an ignorant, powerful cult.

Redhand's horse turned and turned in the wide sunstruck yard. They had opened the gates for him, but none had greeted him. His little crowd looked around themselves, silent, waiting for an order.

"You." Redhand called a grizzled man who stared openly at him. "Call your captain."

"Indisposed."

"How, indisposed?"

The soldier only stared at Redhand, grinning with sunlight, or at a private joke; chewing on a sliver of

bone. Then he turned and went to climb worn stairs
toward the slit of a doorway. Even as he approached it a
man came from the darkness within, armed, helmeted.

"Younger!" Redhand dismounted, went to meet his
brother. Younger came toward him down the stairs,
unsmiling; his eyes had the blank, inward look of a
child just wakened from a nightmare. Without a word
he embraced his brother, clung to him tightly. In the
grip of his embrace, Redhand felt fear.

He pulled himself away, experimented with a friendly
smile, a slap on the shoulder, a laugh of greeting.
Younger reacted to the slap as though stung, and the
laugh died in Redhand's throat.

He turned to Fauconred. "Can you . . ." He waited
for Fauconred to pull his gaze from Younger's face.
"Can you find lodging, stabling? You'll get no help, I
think." Fauconred nodded, glanced once at Younger,
and began to shout orders to the men behind him.

Redhand put an arm tentatively, gently around
Younger's shoulders. "Brother," he said. "Brother." Younger
made no response, only sheltered himself, as he ever
had in his great griefs, within the circle of Redhand's
arm. "Come inside."

He walked with Younger toward the door he had
come out of. All around them the garrison and its
hangers-on looked on, some grinning, some fearful. His
brother had been baited, Redhand knew. It had been so
before; and always Redhand had hit out at them, beaten
at their grinning, stupid faces, so much more mad-
seeming than his brother's. And he would again, he
vowed, memorizing the mockers, unappeased by his
knowledge that they knew no better.

At the cairn, Younger stopped, staring, all his senses
focused there as a rabbit's on a fox in hiding. "In
winter," he began, in a thin, dreaming voice.

"Yes."

"In winter the ground was frozen."

"And."

"He lay still. Now . . ."

"He?"

"Father. Where they buried him. The ground was frozen hard, and he couldn't get out. Now he would push through. He must not, though; no, though he pleads with me." He started suddenly, staring at the pile, and it was as though Redhand could feel a surge of fear through the arm he held his brother with.

"It was Harrah's son," Younger said.

"Harrah?"

"Harrah's son who saw him slain. Harrah's son who threw him in a shallow hole, far too shallow, so shallow the birds would come and peck and scratch the ground. Harrah's son, that Father would get out to go find, but must not, must not . . ."

"Harrah's son," Redhand said slowly, "is dead. I have killed him."

Younger turned to him slowly. He took Redhand's arm in a mad, steel grip. "Dead." Tears of exhausted anguish rose in his eyes. "Then why do the stones move always? *Why does he squirm? Why will he not lie still?*"

In Rennsweek when he was ten years old it had begun, this way: when the vine flowers bloomed on the walls of Old Redhand's house, Younger had poured a child's pailful of dirt on his father's sleeping face, because, he said, tears in his eyes, anyone could see the man was dead . . .

Night along the Edge was cold even in Rennsweek. A fire had been lit; it was the huge room's only light. It lit Younger, who stared into it, lit lights within his eyes, though to Redhand it seemed he looked through his brother's eyes, and the lights he saw were flames within.

"There was a duel," Redhand said. "A kind of duel, with carving knives, in the banquet hall at Redsdown. I killed him. Then I fled."

Impossible to judge if Younger heard or understood.

He only looked into the fire, flames gesturing within his eyes.

"Now I need you, Younger."

Always it had been that the faction that commanded a garrison of the Edge could forge it into a weapon for its use. After the battle at Senlinsdown in the old days, Black Harrah returned from Forgetful without orders to do so, with an unruly army and a new big wife for the King, and the Reds who had thought the King to be in their pockets backed away.

"The King Red Senlin's Son," Redhand said, "was Young Harrah's lover. He will send an army to invest Forgetful, once he deduces I am here. I would prevent that."

Yes, and Red Senlin too, Redhand thought. *He* had gone away to the Edge to be vice-regent then, and in his time *he* had returned with bought Outland chiefs and an army of Edge-outcast soldiers. And Black Harrah had turned and fled . . . Suddenly Redhand felt caught up in the turnings of an old tale, a tale for children, endlessly repetitious. Well, what other chance had he but to repeat what his fathers and their fathers had done? He would not wait here to be ferreted like a rabbit.

"I want to march first, Younger. I want you with me. Help me now, as ever I have done for you."

Younger said nothing, did not turn from the fire.

There was this flaw in it then. The old tale stopped here, the teller faltered at this turning.

That mob in the courtyard was no army. Fauconred had had to cut off some bandit's ear in order to find lodging for Redhand's household. He could flog them into order, a kind of order, with like means if he had weeks in which to do it. He did not have weeks.

"If flesh were stone," said Younger. "If all flesh were stone . . ."

No. He couldn't anyway face the King and the Folk with such a band. Outlanders, and men like these, had no strictures such as the Protectorate had concerning the Folk; they would take what they could. He must draw the country Defenders to his banners, keep the City open to him. It could not be done with marauders.

And they would not flock with any will to himself. He had no true friends; his strength lay in pacts, alliances, sealed with largesse. Red Senlin's Son had seen that, and vitiated it with his City courtiers and his own largesse.

There must be another banner to ride Inward with than his own.

"Her spies," Younger said, smiling. "The messages they take her. Songs, lies, jokes. What harm is there in that?"

With an instant, horrid clarity Redhand remembered the last time he had seen her: at the Little Lake, in the bloody snow, shuffling away on her big horse, riding Outward, looking back for fear.

No!

She must have had the child. Black Harrah's, doubtless. As he had said to Red Senlin (so long ago it seemed) that didn't matter. All the Outlands and half the world would kneel to kiss Little Black's heir.

No!

A joining of Red and Black. An end to the world's anguish. Despite his promises, the King had seized lands, divided them among his friends, who played in the City while farms rotted. The Downs would be his. And the City—well. He had been master of the City. He had friends. It would do.

No! No!

"What harm is there in it?" Younger said again, his voice beginning to quaver.

Redhand took hold of his revulsion and with an effort wrung its neck, stilling its protest. "No harm, brother," he said. "Can you find one of these spies? Do you know them?"

"I know them. Oh, I know them all."

"Send for one. Have him brought here. I . . . have a little joke myself to tell the Queen."

Younger returned to staring into the fire. "Only . . ."

"Only?"

"We will go Inward. But." He turned to Redhand. "Father *must not come!*" He beat his palm against the chair arm with each word. "They said he suffered from a soldier's melancholy. They said, the Endwives said, that spring would bring him round, and they would nurse him back to health. But those were lies."

As in one of the new pageants the King had caused to be shown in the City, the madman in the courtyard of Forgetful had an audience, an audience though of only one; and unlike those pageants' actors, he was unaware of being watched, for the drama unfolding within him took all his attention.

On the belvedere above, his brother, his audience, was attentive, though feeling he had lost the thread, the point, the plot; he shivered in the warm wind, dislocated, lost, feeling that at any moment some unexpected shock might happen. He leaned against the belvedere, tense with expectation, bored with awful expectation.

Now unlike those City pageants, this audience had an audience himself.

Again, an audience of one.

Only she knew the plot. This scene had been laid out in cards the troubled man she watched had never seen; it was a scene in a story begun she knew not how many millennia before she lived, whose end might come as long after her death; she only knew her part, and prayed now to many gods that she might play it right.

From a pouch beneath her cloak of no color she drew the Gun named Suddenly. She was behind a thick pillar of duncolored stone. There were stairs at her back. Beyond, Outward, yellow clouds encircled the setting sun like courtiers around a dying Red king, and as the

sun set, the war-viols of Forgetful would start, calling
the garrison to meat and meeting. She hoped the noise
would cover Suddenly's voice. Afterwards, she would
go quickly down those stairs, down to the stables, to
Farin's black horse she had come to love, without, she
hoped, arousing more suspicion than she had already.
And after that—well: she didn't know. Nightfall. A
curtain on this scene. She scarcely cared, if this was all
played right.

She didn't know either that she, who watched the
madman's audience, had herself an audience. Pageants
upon pageants: she was observed.

He had come up the narrow stair to find his master.
Had seen her at the top of the stair, dim, a blue shadow
in the evening light. When she drew the thing from
within her clothes, he at first did not recognize it; stood
unmoving while a chain of associations took place within him.

So for a moment they all stood motionless; he on the
stair, she with the Gun, he on the belvedere, he below
biting his nails, and also he headless within the incon-
stant earth.

Then the one on the stair ran up.

She didn't know who or what had seized her, only
that its strength was terrible. A hand was clamped over
her face, she could not cry out or breathe; an arm
encircled her, tight as iron bands, pressing the Gun
against her so that if she fired she shot herself. She was
picked up like a bundle of no weight, and before she
was trundled away fast down the stair she saw that the
man on the belvedere still looked down: he had not
seen or heard.

They went quickly down. At a dim turning they
paused; her captor seemed unsure. They turned down a
tunnel-like hall, but stopped when the sound of men
came from far off; turned back, slipped within a niche
formed by the meeting of vast pillars, and waited.

She was beginning to faint; she could not breathe,

and where the arm held her the pain had faded to a
tingling numbness. Sheets of blank blackness came and
went before her eyes. She tasted blood; the pressure of
his hand had cut her mouth on her teeth.

When those coming up the hall had passed without
seeing them, she was rushed out and down again. She
saw evening light spilling from a door at the tunnel's
end, and then it was extinguished, and she knew nothing for a time.

The thud of a door closing woke her. She woke
gulping air, looking into a bald, blank face hooded in
red, oddly calm. Its thin lips moved, and the words
came as from a distance. "You won't cry out, struggle."

"No."

"If they found you. If I gave you to them, they would
hang you."

"Yes. I won't." He was not "they," then?

His face withdrew. Her thudding heart slowed its
gallop, and involuntarily she sighed a long, shuddering
sigh.

The room was tiny, higher almost than wide; above
her head a small window showed a square of summer
evening; there was no other light. A wooden door, small
and thick. A plain wooden pallet she lay on. A wooden
chair he sat in; in one hand he held Suddenly by its
barrel, loosely, as though it were a spoon.

"You are Just," he said.

"If you drop that," she said, her voice still hoarse,
"they will know soon enough you have me."

He lifted the Gun, examined it without curiosity.
"Does it have a name?"

"Why do you keep me?" she said. "I know you, I
know you are a thing of his." She hoped to probe him,
see if there was some disloyalty, some grudge she could
play on . . . His face, though, remained expressionless.
the same mask she had seen always beside Redhand in
the City that spring. Who was he, then?

"I was told they have names."

"They do."

"I have an interest in names."

As though they had gathered here for some scholarly chat. She almost smiled. "And so what is yours?"

"I am called Secretary now."

"That's no name."

"No. I have no other."

She could not read him. There was nothing to grasp. His voice, cool and liquid, the strange nakedness of his face. His hideous strength. For the first time since he had seized her, she felt fear; yet could not imagine how to plead with him, beg him, felt that he knew nothing of mercy. A cold sweat sprang out on her forehead.

"I will say a name," he said, "if I can, and you will tell me if you know it."

What name? Some other she had slain? Some brother or sister? She would tell him nothing...

"Here is the name." It seemed to take all his strength to say it. "Leviathan."

She only looked at him in disbelief.

"Leviathan," he said again. "Do you know that name?"

Evening had deepened. The red cloak he wore was dark now as dried blood; his pale head shone like wax. And as it grew darker in the room, his eyes seemed to glow brighter, as precious stones do.

"Yes." In a whisper.

"Where he lives," the dark form said. "Where he lives, who he is, how to come to him."

He could not mean this; he must be mad.

And yet. "Yes." Again a whisper; he leaned forward to hear. "Yes, I know."

Slowly, as though not meaning to, he leveled Suddenly at her. "Do you pull this? The lever here? And it will kill you?"

She pressed herself against the stone wall behind her, but could not press through it.

"Listen to me," he said, the voice calm, liquid. "I will give you this choice. Take me to this one you know of, wherever, however far Outward. I will give you back this. If you refuse, tell me now, and I will kill you with it."

There was an old story she knew: a brother was surrounded by King's men, who closed in upon him with torches and dogs; he was utterly lost, yet had to escape. He did this, they say: he took a step Outward, a step Inward, and a step away, out and gone. The King's men when they closed the circle found only themselves; they never found him, nor did the Just ever see him again.

She took the step. "Yes. I'll take you. If we leave tonight. I'll take you to see him, I swear it, face to face."

THREE

■

RECORDER

1

How many skills he had learned since that distant morning on the Drum when with the young Endwife he had learned to say Cup and Drink! If there were wonder in him he would have wondered at it.

With Redhand he had learned secrecy, the gaining of ends unknown to others by means devised to seem other than they were. It was not a mode that suited him; he had this failing, a curiosity about others that made it hard for him to keep himself secret. Yet he had this virtue: it all meant little to him but the learning, and he never betrayed himself by eagerness or need.

Never till now.

For this mission was his only. No one had assigned it to him, as Caredd had the watching of her husband, or Redhand the keeping close of his alliances. This he had found within himself, this was the engine of his being, and he had used force and cunning and even the betrayal of his trust to Redhand to accomplish it.

And he feared for its success.

There were winds blowing in him then, awful winds he could hardly bear: this, he thought, is what they all feel, this singularity, this burden of unknown quest, that drives all else out, obscures other loyalties, causes their eyes and thoughts to drift away in conversation, their attention to wander: a mission, whose shape they cannot perceive, whose end they fear for, an end that may be a means, they don't know, or a lie, and yet they have no other.

He thought that in this he had become as fully a man as any of them. It gave him joy, and fear; a fierce resolution, and a strange vacillation he had known nothing of before.

He had stolen. Food from the kitchens, money from the purse he carried for Redhand, good boots and a lamp and a shelter from the quartermaster, a long knife and a short one. He would have stolen horses, but she said they would be useless till far beyond.

He had left the ravished purse and its papers for Redhand, without explanation—had thought to leave a note saying he was returning to the stars, but did not—and had crept away then with the girl, at midnight. Away from his master and the trusts given him. Away from the intrigues he had had some part in directing. Away from Younger's very instructive madness. Away from Forgetful's Outward wall, carrying the girl Nod on his back and her Gun in his belt, down the blind nighttime cliffs of the Edge, ever down, till dawn came and the girl slept and predatory birds circled the ledge they lay on, startled perhaps to see wingless ones there.

From there on the ledge at morning he looked over the Outlands, smoky with mist and obscured by coils of cloud. The paths of meandering rivers were a denser white than the greenshadowed land, which stretched flat and foggy to a great distance; far off the mists seemed to thicken into sky and gray rains could be seen moving like pale curtains in a wind. Except where low hills humped their backs above the mist, it was all shrouded. He woke her, they ate, and continued down.

He imagined this to be like his progress was from sky

to earth, though he could remember nothing of that. As they went downward the air seemed to thicken, the sun's clarity was dimmed, the smooth-faced rocks became slippery with moss and the stone ground began to crumble into earth, sandy at first and cut with flood beds, and then darker and bound by vegetation.

By evening on the second day they were within the Outlands, up to their knees in its boggy grasp.

Late in the night Nod awoke, forgetting where she was, how she had come to be there. She sat upright in the utter darkness, hearing animal noises she did not recognize. Something very close to her grunted, and she inhaled sharply, still half asleep. Then the lamp came bright with a buzzing sound, and his familiar naked face, calm and inquisitive, was looking at her.

"Do we go on now?" he asked.

She blinked at him. "Do you never sleep?"

There was a halo of moisture around the lamp's glow, and clumsy insects knocked against it.

"How far is it?"

"Many days. Weeks." How would she know? How far is it to heaven, how long is death? There were a thousand spirits Nod believed in, prayed to, feared. Yet if someone had said to her, Let's go find the bogey who lives in the lake or the dryad of the high woods, she would have laughed. All that lay in some other direction, on a path you could put no foot on, somewhere at right angles to all else. If they wanted *you*, they would find you.

And perhaps then Leviathan wanted this one. Perhaps he walked that path, perhaps he was at right angles to all else.

"It will be dawn soon," he said.

Yes. That was it; and in spite of what they had agreed, *he* led *her*: to the edge of the world, to look over the edge, and call into the Deep.

Through the morning, mist in wan rags like unhappy ghosts rose up from the Outlands, drawn into the sun, but still lay thick along the river they followed. Gray trees with pendulous branches waded up to their knobby knees in the slow water.

"We must go up," she said. "We have to have dry ground, though we lose the way Outward." That she knew, that the rivers flowed Outward here as they flowed Inward on the other side of the Edge. But they would have to find another marker, or spend a lifetime in mud here.

They had begun to decide which way was up when the Secretary stopped still, listening. She stopped too, could hear nothing, and then sorted from the forest's murmur the knock of wood on wood, the soft slosh of water around a prow. A sound she knew well.

The Outlanders she had known were dour merchants she had ferried to the City, resplendent for the occasion but awed too: she had felt superior to them in her City knowledge. Here it was otherwise, and she sank behind the knees of a great tree. The Secretary followed; she was, after all, the guide.

The boat sounds grew closer, though they could see nothing through the shroud of mist; and then there came, walking on the water it seemed, a tall, tall figure, hideously purple of face with staring eyes . . . It took them a moment to see it was the boat's carved prow.

Dark men with long, delicate poles sounded the river channel, and called softly back to those who rowed. Deep-bellied, slow, with tiny banners limp in the windless air, it passed so close they could hear the oarsmen grunt, and its wake lapped their feet. Yards of it went by, each oarhole painted as a face with the oar its tongue, and each face looked at them unseeing.

In the stern, stranger than all the painted faces, there was a woman under a pavilion, a vast woman, a woman deep-bellied like the ship. She lay cushioned in her fat, head resting on an arm like a thigh, fast asleep. At her feet, in diverse attitudes, Outlanders, chiefs with brass spangles braided in their beards, slept too; one held to his softly heaving chest a grotesque battle-ax.

The boat passed with a soft sound, rolled slightly with the channel, which made the Queen list too, and was lost in the mist.

Other boats came after, not so grand but stuffed full of armed men, spiky and clanking with weapons. One by one they appeared and glided by. Deep within one boat, someone chuckled.

"Is the child strong?" Redhand asked. "Healthy? Is it male or female?"

The Queen said nothing, only continued with her refreshment. Before her was a plate like a tray, tumbled up in Outland fashion with cakes, fruits, cheese, and fat sausages.

"I would see the child," Redhand said.

"There are other things," the Queen said, "that must come first."

She was waited on by a lean, fish-eyed man, her companion and general, a man named Kyr: Redhand and he had exchanged names, looked long in each other's faces, both trying to remember something, but neither knew that it was Kyr who had nearly killed Redhand at the Little Lake. Kyr passed to his mistress a napkin; she took it, her eyes on her food.

So they waited—Redhand; Fauconred, who looked red-faced and furious as though he had been slapped; and Younger Redhand.

It had been an awful week. Redhand, with Fauconred's help, had locked his screaming brother in a tower room, at dead of night so no one saw. Then he had ordered the cairn in the courtyard dismantled.

He dug out of the garrison an unshaven, wispy man who said he was Gray, made him presentable, and then, with him presiding, had Old Redhand exhumed from the courtyard. He forced himself to look on, his jaw aching with nights of sleepless resolve; he made the garrison look on too, and they did, silent and cowed before his ferocity and his father's mortality.

He had found a quiet chamber within Forgetful, that once may have been a chapel, with dim painting on one wall he could not read, of a smiling, winged child perhaps; it would do. He had the great stones of the floor torn up, and a place made. From the dark wood of old chests a carpenter of his household had made a box.

"Wine," the Queen said. "No water."

When the last of the floor stones had been mortared back into place, and the same carpenter had tried an inscription on them, two or three ancient letters only that would stand for the rest, Redhand went to the tower and released Younger. Hesitant, his cheeks dirty with dried tears, Younger allowed himself to be taken and shown the empty place in the courtyard, and the quiet room and its secure stones. *Now*, Redhand had said, gripping his brother's shoulders, *now you have no more excuse to be mad. Please. Please* . . . They had embraced, and stood for a while together, and Redhand from exhaustion and confused love had wept too.

Whatever it was, the true burial, or Redhand's strength in doing this, or only that the vine flowers fell in that week: the horrid surgery worked. Younger slept for a day, worn out by his adventure, and woke calm: well enough to sit with his brother and Fauconred now, somewhat stunned, with the look of one returned from a long and frightening journey.

Kyr poured water from a ewer over the Queen's fingers, and only when she had dried them did she look up, with her marvelous eyes, at her new allies. "Have this cleared," she said, gesturing with a ringed hand at her pillaged feast, "and we will talk."

There had been little time for Redhand to worry over his Secretary and his weird disappearance, though now he felt in need of him. The man, if man he had been, was so fey that in a sense Redhand felt he had not ever been truly there: this though he had saved Redhand's life, twice. Well, there was no help for it. Redhand felt less that he had lost a friend or even an aide than that he had misplaced a charm, lucky but possibly dangerous too.

"Now, lady," Redhand said.

"We have conditions," she said. "We have drawn them up, you and whoever else will sign them."

"Conditions."

"Certain incomes I demand. Honors restored. There is a house near Farinsdown I wish for my summers." She took a paper from Kyr. "There are names here of those I want punished."

"Punished?"

"Much wrong was done me." As though it were a morsel, her fat hands unrolled the paper lovingly. "Red Senlin's Son, I have him here, and he must die."

"So must we all." Something like a smile had begun to cross Redhand's features. "Who else have you?"

She let the paper curl itself again, her dark eyes suspicious. "There are others."

"Half the Red Protectorate?"

"I will have revenge."

Redhand began to laugh, a hoarse, queer laugh that he owed to his old wound, and over his laughter the Queen's voice rose: "I will have revenge! They murdered Black Harrah, they imprisoned my husband, they took my crown, they killed my child!"

Redhand stopped laughing. "Your child."

The Queen stared at him defiantly.

"Where is the child?" he asked.

She rose slowly, raised her head, proud. "There is no child," she said quietly. "Red Senlin murdered him."

"Murdered a *child*?"

"His relentlessness. His constant harassment. I miscarried on the Drum."

Redhand too rose, and came toward the Queen, so malevolent that Kyr stepped close. "You have no child," Redhand said. "Then tell me, Lady, what you do here with your conditions, and your demands, and your revenges. Do you think we owe you now, any of us, anyone in the world? For your beauty only, did you think?"

She did not shrink, only batted her black lashes.

"These," he said, flicking her papers, hoarse with rage, "these will be our reason then to cross the Drum? Answer me, Lady. To kill the King, and any else who might have mocked you once or done you wrong?"

"No, Redhand."

"What reason, then?"

"To free my husband from the house they have prisoned him in. Free Little Black, and make him King again."

Redhand turned away, flung himself in his chair. But he said nothing.

"Send to the Black Protectorate," the Queen said. "Send word that you mean to do this. He has always been their King. They will rise."

Redhand glared at nothing, his jaw tight.

"It is your only hope, Redhand."

"The old man may be dead, or mad," Fauconred said.

"He is not dead. I have spies near him. And he is no more mad than he ever was."

"When the King learns of it," Redhand growled, "he will kill Little Black. It surprises me he has not yet."

The Queen sat heavily. "He will not learn of it. Send word to Blacks only, I will say whom, they will not reveal it. To your Red friends say only you want their help. Put it about that the child lives."

Redhand slowly shook his head.

"The notion brought me you," the Queen said lightly. "And before Red Senlin's Son learns that you mean anything but to save yourself, Little Black will be with us. I have people, Redhand, in the City, who have planned his escape, are ready to pluck Little Black from that awful place at my word."

"I have no faith in this," Redhand said.

"Nor I," said Fauconred.

The Queen's eyes lit fiercely. "Then you tell me, exiles, outlaws, what other chance you have. What other hope."

There was a long silence. Far away, from the courtyard, they could hear a fragment of an Outland song. Redhand, sunk in thought, looked less like a man weighing chances than one condemned reconciling himself. At last he said, almost to himself: "We will go Inward, then."

The Queen leaned forward to hear him. "Inward?"

"Send word to your people. Free the King, if you can."

She leapt up, flinging up her arms, and began a vast dance. "Inward! Inward! Inward!" She lunged at the table, reaching for her papers. "The conditions..."

"No."

"You must sign them."

"No. No more. Leave that."

She turned on them in fury. "You will sign them! Or I return!"

"Yes!" Redhand hissed. "Yes, go back to your bogs and lord it over your villages, weep storms over your wrongs. I will have no vengeance done. None." He raised his arm against her. "Pray to all your gods you are only not hanged for this. Make no other conditions."

"My incomes," she said, subdued. "What is due me."

"*If* this succeeds," Redhand said, "you will be treated as befits the King's loved wife. But all direction, now and hereafter, will be mine."

"You would be King yourself."

"I would be safe. And live in a world that does not hate me. You find that hard to grasp."

She rolled up her papers. "Well, for now. We will talk further of this."

"We will not." He turned to leave her; Fauconred and Younger stood to follow.

"Redhand," she said. "There is one further thing." Regal, on feet strangely small, she made progress toward them as though under sail. "You must kneel to me."

"Kneel!" Fauconred said.

"You must kneel, out there, before them all, or I swear I will return."

"Never, he never will," Younger whispered.

She only regarded them, waiting for her due. "Kneel to me, kneel and kiss my hand, swear to be my defender."

Fauconred, and Younger with his whipped boy look, waited. Redhand, with a gesture as though he were wiping some cloud from before his eyes, only nodded.

It all took so long, he thought. So terribly long. Life is brief, they said. But his stretched out, tedious, difficult, each moment a labor of unutterable length. He wished suddenly it might be over soon.

Of all hard things Sennred had ever borne, imprisonment seemed the hardest. Adversity had never hurt him, not deeply; he seemed sometimes to thrive on it. The mockery of children at his misshapenness had made him not hard but resilient; death and war had made him the more fiercely protective of what he loved; the intrigues of his brother's brilliant court had made him not quick and brittle as it had the Son, but slow, long-sighted, tenacious. Though he was young, younger by years than the young King, Sennred had nothing left in him impetuous, half-made, loud.

What marked him as young was his love. He gave it, or withheld it, completely and at once. He had given it to his brother, and to Redhand. And then lastly to a young wife with autumn eyes and auburn hair, a free gift, without conditions, a gift she knew nothing of yet.

And what galled him in imprisonment, made him

rage, was to be separated from those he loved, deprived of his watching over them; he could not conceive they could get on without him, it blinded him with anxiety that they were in danger, threatened, taking steps he could not see.

Where they had put him he could hardly see if it was night or day.

As though it were a maze made for the exercise of some small pet, most of the great house he had been shut in had been sealed off. The rest, windowless, doorless, he had his way in. It had been a Black mansion in some ancient reign; there were high halls where ghostly furniture still held conference, moldering bedrooms, corridors carved and pillared where his footsteps multiplied and seemed to walk toward him down other carved corridors. For days on end he went about it with candles cadged from his guards, exploring, looking he was not sure for what: a way out, an architectural pun somewhere that would double out suddenly and show him sky, blue and daylit.

His companions were a woman who brought food, deaf and evil-smelling—he thought sometimes her odor had got into his food, and he couldn't eat—and his guards, whom he would meet in unexpected places and times. He seemed rarely to see the same guard twice, and could not tell if there were multitudes of guards or if they were only relieved often. Anyway they were all huge, leather-bound, dull and seemingly well-paid; all he could get from them were candles, and infrequently a jug of blem, after which he would go around the great rooms breaking things and listening to the echoes.

And there was the ghost.

He had at first been a glimpse only, a shadow at the far edge of vision, and Sennred never saw more of him than a flick of robe disappearing around a corner. But the ghost seemed to delight in following him, and they began a game together through the dayless gloom of the house; Sennred supposed the ghost suffered as much from strangulating boredom as he did.

Natural enough that such a place would have a ghost, though Sennred suspected that this one was at least a little alive. Nor had it taken him long to deduce whose ghost it might be. He would have asked the guards, but he was afraid they would make new arrangements, and his only relief from the torment of imprisonment was his plan to catch this other one.

His trap was laid.

He had found a low corridor, scullery or something, with doors at each end of its lefthand wall. He learned that these were both doors of a long closet that ran behind the wall the length of the corridor. He learned he could go in the far door, double back through the closet, taking care not to stumble on the filthy detritus there, and come out the other door, just behind anyone who had followed him into the corridor.

Once he had discovered this, he had only to wait till his ghost was brave enough to follow him there. As near as he could measure time, it was a week till he stood listening at his trapdoor for soft, tentative footsteps . . .

When he judged they had just passed him, he leapt out with a yell, filthy with cobwebs, and grappled with his ghost.

He had a first wild notion that it was truly a ghost, a greasy rag covering only a bundle of bones; but then he turned it to face him, and looked into the face he had expected, wildeyed, the mouth open wide in a sound-less scream.

"Your Majesty," Sennred said.

"Spare me!" said the King Little Black in a tiny voice. "Spare me for right's sake!"

"And what will you give me?"

"What you most want," said the ghost.

"Freedom," Sennred said. "Freedom from this place. With the power of your crown, old man, grant me that."

*   *   *

He was old, and lived by lizard hunting. Perhaps the bloodstained boat was all his living; the Secretary, anyway, didn't think of that, though he did perceive the old man's terror when they appeared before him as though risen out of the mud. The coins they gave him must have been nearly useless to him; it didn't matter, they had been ready after days of mud to wrest the boat from him if need be, and the old one knew that.

The Secretary turned back once to look at him as the girl poled off. He stood unblinking, wrinkled as a reptile, his old claw clutching the gold .

Nod had long ago given up any idea of overpowering her captor, seizing the Gun from him, murdering him by stealth. Even to slip away, leaving the Gun, though it would have been like losing a limb, even that she had abandoned; he slept only when she slept, and her slightest stirring woke him.

So she went Outward, days into weeks, in a weird dream, the half dream the sleeper seems to know he dreams, and struggles restlessly to wake from. Yet she could not wake. Waking, she poled the boat. Sleeping, she dreamt of it.

It seemed they moved through the interior of some vast organism. It was dark always, except at high noon when a strange diffracted sunlight made everything glisten. The trees hung down ganglia of thick moss into the brown river slow with silt; the river branched everywhere into arteries clogged with odorous fungi and phosphorescent decay. At night they lay in their shelter listening to the thing gurgling and stirring.

They came once upon a place where a fresh spring had come forth in the scum and decay, like a singer at a funeral. The spring had swept clean a little lagoon, and even bared a few rocks of all but a slimy coat of algae.

She swam, dappled by sun through the clotted leaves.

He had some notion, abstract only, of men's bodies and their heats and functions, and had stored up court gossip and jokes to be explicated later. He watched her, faintly curious. She was made not unlike himself.

She wriggled up onto the rocks, laughing, brushing the water from her face, pale and glistening as a fish.

She saw him watching. "Turn away," she said sternly, and he did.

When at last the forest began to thin, and the tree trunks stood up topless and rotted like old teeth, and the rivers merged into a shallow acrid lake that seemed to have drowned the world, they had lost track of what week it was.

"Why are there no people?" His voice was loud in the utter silence. "Shouldn't there be villages, towns?"

"I don't know."

"There are Outlanders."

"Yes."

"Where?"

"Elsewhere."

"Do you know where we are?"

"No."

There was no line between water and sky; it was all one gray. The hooded sun burned dimly Inward, and a light like it burned within the lake.

There were no trees here; perhaps the shelf of the world below had grown too thin to contain their roots. There were only bunches of brown weed that stood up leafless and sharp, with a silver circle of wake around each stem. Only by these weeds could they tell their little boat moved at all.

They could see far off to their right a moving smudge of pink on the water. It rose up, settled again. Then a long boat gray as the lake crept from the weeds out there, and gray men with nets attached to long poles began to snare the pink birdlets that had floated away from the flock. When one was snared it cried out, and the pink clot rose, and then settled again nearby.

"Quickwings too stupid to fly all away," Nod said. It was the first time she had spoken that day, except to answer him.

"You will speak to them. Ask them . . ."

"No."

"Ask them . . ."

"I will not, not, not!" She looked around her, looking for escape, but there was only gray water, gray sky, indifferent, featureless. She sat down suddenly in the bows and began to weep.

He only stared at her, long hands on his knees, mystified.

Far off where the nets moved quick as birds in the gloom, men turned and pointed at their boat.

The birdmen had made themselves an island on that placeless lake; it was a raft, anchored to the bottom, an acre of lashed beams, platforms, rotten wood. All night the quickwings they had caught that day fluttered within long cages of wicker and string; all night the lake oozed up through the ancient beams of the raft. So old and big it was, their raft grew little groves of mushrooms, and fish lived out their lives amid the sheltering fronds that grew from its bottom. It was to this island they brought Nod and the Secretary, not quite prisoners, yet not quite guests either.

All night the one-eyed birdman sat next to Nod, talking in a language she didn't understand. He would slip off into the dark and return with some token, a stone, a rag of figured, moldered cloth, a lizard's tooth.

She told herself he wasn't there. She sat with her knees up, trying to clean from her feet the inexplicable sores that had begun to appear there.

She glanced up now and again; far off, in the muddy light of a lantern, the Secretary sat talking with some of them. They gestured, stood, pointed, sat again. He listed, unmoving. She had the idea he understood no more of their talk than she did.

When the one-eyed birdman, with a sudden gesture, slipped his moist hands beneath her clothes, she rose, furious, and made her way over incomprehensible bundles and slimy decks to where the Secretary sat, looking Outward.

"Protect me," she whispered fiercely, "or give me back my Gun."

Dawn was a gray stain everywhere and nowhere.

"Do you hear? I am helpless here. I hate it. Are you a man?"

"There." He pointed Outward. A light that might have been marshlight flickered far away and disappeared. "There. The last house in the world, they said; and the one who lives there has spoken to Leviathan."

2

The tower of Inviolable may be the highest place in the world. No one has measured, but no one knows a higher place.

There are many rooms in the tower, scholars' rooms, put there less for the sublimity of the height than in the Order's belief that men who spend their lives between pages should at least climb stairs for their health. Because Inviolable has no need for defense, the tower is pierced with broad windows, and the windows look everywhere, down the forests to the lake in the center of the world, a blue smudge of mist on summer mornings. Outward over the Downs where the river Wanderer branches into a hundred water fingers, to the Drum and farther still. But when the scholars put down their

pens and look up, their gaze is inward; the vistas they
see are in time not space.

One looks out, though, a slight and softly handsome
man in black, looking for something he probably could
not anyway perceive at this height, this distance... There
is, far off, a tower of dark cloud, a last summer storm
walking Inward across the Drum to thresh the harvest
lands with hail; Learned Redhand can hear the mutter
of its thunder. The storm raises winds around the
world; even here in the forests, wind turns leaves to
show their pale undersides as though it fling handfuls
of silver coins through the trees. It will be here soon
enough. Yes: the Black Protectorate raises an army on
the Black Downs, Redhand's dependents unfurl, however reluctantly, their old battle banners: the storm will
come soon Inward.

Was it this that old Mariadn died to avoid, this the
burden she ordered the Grays never to envy him? Did
she lay it on him only because he deserved to suffer it,
or because she saw something in him that might miti-
gate it, some strength to make a shelter from this
storm? If she did, he cannot find it in himself.

In another tower bells ring, low-voiced and sweet,
reverberating through Inviolable, saying *day's end, day's
end*. Around Learned, books close with the sound of
many tiny doors to secret places, and there is the sound
of speaking for speaking's sake, now that silence has
been lifted. They pass behind Learned on their way
downward, greeting him diffidently, expecting no reply,
Arbiter, Arbiter, good evening, good day, Arbiter, our
thoughts are with you... Against the sound of their
many feet descending the stairs, he hears the sound of
someone ascending; as those going down grow distant,
one comes closer. He is alone now in the tower; the
square of sunlight printed on the wall behind him is
dimming, and the window before him rattles as the
winds begin to enwrap Inviolable.

The unquestioning affection, the sincere hopes of his

scholars, he knows to be less for him than for the black he wears; though, perhaps, by the end of his lifelong Arbitration, he may earn it for himself. Or they may call him, as they do some others of ancient times, a white Arbiter, foolish, useless to the world.

Or worse, a Red.

No. Not ever that.

A bone-white Gray at last achieves the room Learned sits in and comes to him, hesitant, unwilling to break Learned's meditation.

"Yes? Come in. What is it?"

"There is a rider below, Arbiter, all in red leather."

"I have expected him, I suppose."

"He says he comes from your brother the Protector. He brings you this."

It is a small piece of scarlet ribbon tied in a complex knot.

"Tell him to wait," Learned says, turning the ribbon in his fingers, "and see my carriage is made ready to travel."

Later that night, in a secret place in the forest far below Inviolable, white hands laid out cards on a board within a painted tent. The Neither-nor shivered, and the lamp flame too, when wind discovered the tent's hiding-place and made the tent-cloths whisper; but it was not only the wind that made the Neither-nor shiver.

For the seventh time It had turned down the card that bore an image of Finn: a death's head, with a fire burning in his belly, and this motto: *Found by the lost*.

The Neither-nor had chosen the card Roke to be the girl whose name was called Nod; and Roke should fall in some relation to the card Caermon, who was Redhand; should fall with the trump Rizna between, It had hoped. But Caermon hid within the pack, and Finn fell. Odd.

Where was Nod?

Dead . . . no; the cards did not seem to say so. Gone, lost. Anyway, her task remained undone, that was clear. Redhand hid. The Neither-nor snapped the Roke card's edge against the board.

The wind, with a sudden gust like a hand, picked up the tent's door flap. Outside, clouds raced across the Wanderers, or the Wanderers raced, it could not be said which; the forest, opulent in the windy darkness, gestured toward the Neither-nor's door.

Someone was coming up the secret way toward the Neither-nor's tent.

With a sudden rush of feeling, the Neither-nor thought it to be Nod. But in another moment the figure became a man, a boy really, who did look like the girl Nod. His name was called Adar, the Neither-nor remembered: a name chosen for great things.

As the Neither-nor had partly suspected, Adar had come to ask after the girl.

"No word, no word."

"The cards . . ."

"Silent, confused it may be."

They sat together as though afloat; the tent-cloths filled like sails, and the forest creaked and knocked and whispered continuously. The Neither-nor began to lay out cards, aimlessly, hardly watching, while the boy talked.

"The King has begun a tomb in the City. A hundred artisans are at work on it. He plays with this while the Queen gathers strength."

Doth, Haspen, Shen. Barnol, Ban, the trump Tintinnar, Roke and Finn again.

"I have watched near Fennsdown. They will not move without the King. Redhand . . ."

The Neither-nor's pack released the card Caermon.

"Redhand." The Neither-nor knew the next card. Adar fell silent. Whatever had become of Nod, whatever the chill card Finn spoke of, at least now It knew the next step.

"Redhand," said Adar, and the Neither-nor laid Rizna reversed before him, Rizna with sickle and seedbag, who constantly reaps what he forever sows.

"It will storm soon," the Neither-nor said. "Sit with me awhile before you go . . ."

All through that night, and through the next day and the next night, the Arbiter's closed black carriage rolled over the world, following the man in red leather.

Once out of the forest, they flew over the streets of Downs villages rain-washed and deserted nearly; along streets cobbled and dirt, past shuttered walls where loud placards of the Just were pasted, that the Folk would not or dared not remove; and on then, past the last cottage lamplit in the dark and stormy afternoon, on Outward.

Inside, the Arbiter, in a wide hat against the dripping from a leak in the roof, his hands on a stick between his knees, listened to the rattle of the fittings and the knocking of the wind against his door. Off and on, he turned over in his mind an old heretical paradox: if a man has two parents, four grandparents, eight great-grandparents, and so on endlessly back to the beginning of time, then how could it be that the world began with only fifty-two?

The carriage rolled; eight, sixteen, thirty-two, sixty-four, a hundred and twenty-eight, two hundred and fifty-six . . . In thirty generations or so the number would be almost beyond counting. And yet the world began with fifty-two . . .

The road went plainly on, wet and silvery between endless low retaining walls of piled fieldstone where rabbits lived. The few Folk left trying to gather in sodden hay in the rain turned to look as he passed.

High in a headland tower that looked out over Redsdown, in a room she never left any more, Mother Caredd sat by the window putting up her fine white hair with many bone pins. Far below her, on the

Outward road, a carriage appeared as if conjured. It topped a rise and seemed to float down into a slough on the rainwings it cast up, and disappeared, only to appear, smaller, further on. She watched it go; it seemed to have some urgent appointment with the black clouds far Outward that the road between stone walls ran toward.

"Hurry," said Mother Caredd, and her servant looked up. "Hurry, hurry."

By nightfall of the next day, the man in red had brought the carriage within a vast circle of watchfires on the Drum, past sentries Red, Black and Outlander, into the Queen's encampment. It looked as though half the world had gone to war.

"And Caredd?" Redhand asked.

"Well. Untroubled. The house is guarded, but she is left in peace. Only she is not allowed to write, not even to me."

It was odd to think of, but Learned had never been within one of his brother's war tents, though his brother had lived as much in tents as he had in houses. It was large, shadowy, hung with tapestries. Rugs covered the Drumgrass underfoot; a charcoal brazier glowed on a tripod. There were chairs, chests, a bed, all cleverly contrived to be folded and carried on wagons. The furnishings seemed ancient, much used, battered like old soldiers. How long and well, Learned thought, we prepare for war, how thoughtfully and lovingly is it fitted out.

"Have you seen the Queen?" Redhand asked.

"No."

"You will wish to."

"No."

Redhand looked up from the papers he studied, pushed them aside. His reading lamp shone on armor, carefully polished, that stood up on a stand beside him like a second Redhand. "Learned." He smiled, his old, genuine smile. "I am grateful. It can't have been a pleasant ride."

"There was time to think."

Redhand got up, and Learned seemed to see for a moment another man, old, weary, to whom even the business of standing and sitting is too much labor. He poured steaming drink for the Arbiter from a pitcher by the brazier. "For the chill of the Drum.

"I would have come to you," he went on, "but I am an outlaw now, my name is posted in the towns like a horse thief's. You understand."

"Yes."

"What we wish of you," he said, turning his mug in his hands, "is simple, and doubtless you have suspected it. We wish only that you retract the decision of the old Arbiter in favor of the Senlin claims, and restore all to Little Black."

"Only."

"Say she was old, incapable. You know the words."

Learned wished suddenly he need not tell his brother what he must; he wished only to listen to that harsh voice, quick with authority. He savored the sound of it, carefully, as though he might never hear it more. "Do you remember," he said, "when first I went away, first put on Gray?"

Redhand smiled shortly. There was much to do.

"That Yearend when I came home, in my new white, so smug; I would take no orders from you, or turn the spit anymore when you said to."

"I remember."

"I was hateful. I bowed to Father, but only in a conditional sort of way. They had told me, you see, that my family had me no more, nor would I ever have any other: the Grays were all, and I owed them all."

"There was something about a horse."

"My painted. You said if I was Gray now, I had no more claim on any Redhand horse."

"We fought."

"Fought! You beat me pitilessly. I was never a fighter."

"Do you forgive me?" Redhand said, laughing.

"More important, brother, dear bully, you must forgive me, now, in advance."

Redhand put down his cup.

"I cannot do what you ask," Learned said softly. Terrible to see him so, stunned, helpless, in the power of a younger brother who had ever followed him. "Redhand, all my powers, resources are yours."

"All but this judgment."

"That is not mine to give. It belongs to Righteousness."

"Pious." He spat out the word. "Pious. When it was all lies, Learned, your judgment, and made at my bidding, at your House's bidding..."

"I know that. Don't go on. I cannot do this."

Redhand sat again. "Will you condemn me?"

"The old judgment stands."

"Call me traitor?"

"Are you not?"

They sat without looking at each other; the hostile silence was palpable between them. Outside, muffled drums marked the watch. Redhand poured cold water on his hands, wiped his face and beard, and sat then with his hands over his face.

"Redhand, if you leave this thing." It was hard to say. "Leave that tripes and her malcontents to their war, then... you will be under my protection. When the Queen is beaten, the King may forgive you. Return you Redsdown..."

Redhand looked up, but not at Learned, at nothing. "And what will I do at Redsdown? Pray?" With his knuckles he struck a gong that hung behind him. The sour sound hung in the tent. "That painted you spoke of. It died only last autumn, after a long life. He was a proud one, and fathered many."

"Yes."

"When we fought, it was because I was afraid you

would have him gelded, and made a Gray's palfrey. You understand."

Two armed men showed themselves at the tent's door.

"Do you still play War in Heaven?" Redhand asked his brother.

"Rarely."

"Well. I have crossed the line, Learned. All my stones are on the board. If I must break rules I will break them. I am gone out to make a king again, and I suppose I can make an arbiter too." He motioned the armed men in. "Take the Arbiter," he said, "to some secure place, and keep him close."

"Redhand, don't do this."

"He shall have all comforts, but let him not escape."

The two men took Learned, tentatively, with respect. He stood, took up his wide hat against the rain outside. "You will have war."

"To the death, mine or his." It scarcely seemed to matter to him which. "It would help me to have this judgment. When you wish to render it, only tell me, and we will send you home." The guards began to lead Learned away. "Wait."

The light of the brazier lit two dull fires beneath Redhand's thick brow. He sat huddled in his camp chair, as though he, not Learned, were the prisoner. "A point of law," he said. "I would make a will. How can I make it so that Caredd will have all, and in safety?"

"I'll consider it," Learned said. "There are ways."

"Thank you."

"And I have a problem for you."

"Yes?"

"If a man has two parents, and four grandparents, eight great-grandparents, and so on back to the beginning of time, how is it then that the world began with fifty-two?"

"Did the world?"

"So it is said."

Redhand regarded him, chewing on his thumbnail. "Do you know the answer?"

"Partly. We three, you and Younger and I, are part of it."

"Well." He put his hand on the papers before him. "I have other problems here."

"Perhaps," Learned said. "Perhaps, Redhand, and perhaps not."

"They will make me King again."

Oh, he was agile; he flew up back stairways Sennred had not known about, in the dark, as if by some other sense overstepping the rotten stairs. He climbed to porticos like a busy spider. Sennred for all his young strength could hardly follow him. No wonder he had eluded Sennred for weeks; no wonder he could communicate with spies the King's men knew nothing of.

Upward they went, climbing the great house as though within a chimney.

At a crack, a window incompletely sealed, a fugitive ray shone in full of golden motes. The King Little Black stopped, and for the twentieth time drew out the paper, much folded, soft as kid skin. He read or spoke by rote the contents quickly: "Fear not, Sir, your deliverance is near. Redhand and the Queen's army is thousands now and the Son is on the march, and when you are with them their hearts will be high and you shall succeed in this. Be where we agreed before, on any night after you have this, we will watch every night, Sir, be quick if you can; we are in great danger here." He folded the note. "You see, you see?"

"Yes. Let's go on."

"You shall be rewarded," the King went on in his tiny voice. "I know the loyal, and you shall have reward. You shall be my minister. You shall see that their heads fall, yes, severed, every one." He paused to pry up a board that sealed the way, that Sennred would have thought immovable; when they had squeezed through, he pulled it carefully back into place. "Redhand, he shall have his neck cut quite through, yes, and Red Senlin too."

He seemed to confuse the war that had unseated him with this one, to want to slay his new allies and resurrect old enemies. It had always been thought that the executions during his reign had been all Black Harrah's doing, because the King had never shown himself. *If only Little Black knew*, the loyal used to say. But Sennred had for days been listening to his grisly tastes. He thought for sure the King had found in those days some secret niche to watch all from.

By a sudden echo of their footsteps in the dark, Sennred could tell that the back stairs had debouched into a wide high place, bare-floored, empty of furniture.

Beneath the smell of must and disuse in the room, there was another odor, intensely familiar to Sennred.

"Stop. Wait awhile."

"Hurry, hurry!"

That smell ... Yes! He was sure now, and he stumbled with his arms outstretched to find the wall, and the racks on the wall he knew must be there ... He stepped into some pieces of armor that rang like bells, and the King gave a frightened squeak.

But Sennred had found what he wanted.

How many hours he had spent in such a room, a room smelling of leather and steel polish, sweat and moldering straw targets, loud with weapons; how much of his life's little happiness he had got there! He gripped the sword's handle gratefully; it was like slipping into warm clothes after having been long naked.

"Lead on, Majesty," he said. "Your minister comes close after."

There was a suffocating hour when they had to crawl up between two close walls of crumbling brick, by elbow and knee and will. The King went scrabbling first, and Sennred pushed him from below, his nose full of the smell of the old man's rusty clothes, hating him fiercely; and then there was a hole in the floor above them, and they crawled out into a tower room windowed and full of breeze.

Air. Light. Stars. Sennred stood panting, wiping the filthy sweat from his face.

They were near the very top of the house, up among its steep-pitched roofs and chimney stacks and fantastic cupolas. Below them the high-piled City was already starred with lamplight; all around, the lake lay like a hole pierced in the Deep.

The house stood outside the High City walls, on a finger of rock called Spring that was connected to the High City by a causeway; down there, watchfires burned, guards stood, they knew. On this side, though, the walls of the house went down and met the sheer walls of the rock Spring which went down, down to the lake and down then to the bottom of the world presumably.

"They will show a lantern," Little Black said. "Down there, where Spring meets the house. There are no guards there; they don't know there is a way there down the rock to the lake." He giggled. "They will know, one day, when they are all flung down Spring one by one. One by one."

"A lantern. And how will we get down to them then?"

"Crawl down, crawl down, swift as anything." He peered out over the window ledge into the gloom. "There are ways. There are handholds."

"And once down..."

"They have a boat, concealed at the bottom on the lake. Over there there is a path up the mountain that meets the High Road." He patted his hands together, gleeful. "And then free! Free!"

Sennred leaned out with the King. "Show me. Point it all out, how you will climb down."

The King's crooked finger traced the way down, along gutters, down roofs, clinging to gargoyles, walking ledges. With the horrid fear already biting into his knees, Sennred memorized it.

"There!" Little Black cried. "There they are!"

Down where the walls of the house met the walls of the rock Spring, a yellow light winked once, again.

Now, shouted all prudence in Sennred's mind, *do it now, here, there will be no other chance....* He gripped the sword, staring at the King's back; the King's matted white hair stirred in the evening wind.

He could not do it; could not raise the sword, could not thrust it within the black cloak. The King turned and grinned wildly at him, and then slipped over the window ledge.

There was nothing for Sennred to do but follow. He didn't even know the way back into his prison.

A tiled roof went steeply down from the tower room, down to a gutter green with verdigris; the King let himself slip down the tiles, like a child at play, and caught himself on the gutter. Sennred, going slower, had a harder time; his caution caught him up on the tiles and nearly flung him into the night. He lay crouched at the gutter, panting, collecting himself. *There is no way,* he thought, *to do this but fearlessly, I will fall otherwise*... He tried to find in himself the fearlessness that the King (whispering urgently to him from around the roof's turning) had as a gift of his foolishness.

It was easier for a while around the roof's turning; they walked through a chute formed by two roofs' meeting, crept around clustered chimneys standing eerie and unconcerned in the moonlight, and stood then looking over a cornice. Here the wall went down sheer; there was only a ladder of stones, outcropping for some obscure mason's reason, that could be descended. With a little grunt of triumph, the King started down. Sennred could only follow because he was sure that he would fall, that caution was useless...

He stepped off the last stone onto a ledge, almost surprised.

They were in a valley between two wings of the house. A narrow chasm separated the ledge they stood on from a symmetrical ledge on the wall opposite; it must be jumped; they could not continue down on this side or they might be seen. The chasm was dark; how far down it went could not be seen, to the bottom of the house or further...

Outward, between the two wings of the house, was a narrow banner of night sky, still faintly green at the horizon but already starred. They could look down that way to the lake and the way that they had been promised was there; and even as they looked down, the yellow light winked again.

Across the chasm, a lizard, a stonecutter's fancy, clung to the wall above the ledge.

"Leap, leap," the King said. "Take hold of that thing when your foot strikes the ledge, and hold yourself to the wall." He prodded Sennred, who stood transfixed, looking down. "No!" the King said. "Look only at that, at that"—waggling his finger at the monster.

Sennred leapt.

His hand took hold of the lizard's foot as his foot took hold of the ledge; a weird sound came from his throat and he clung there a moment, stone himself, till the King's urgings made him let go and edge away.

The King poised himself a moment; his hair stirred in the air that sped through that narrow place; his hands moved like claws. Then he leapt too.

His hand took hold of the lizard's head, and gently, as though made of rotten wood, the head came away.

The King, looking faintly surprised, drifted backwards off the ledge, one hand spooning the air, the other holding the lizard's head as though it were a gift.

Sennred leaned over with a cry, almost falling himself, and snatched at the King's black cloak. It came away in his hand, rolling the King out as from a bag.

He fell soundlessly. It was Sennred who screamed, not knowing he did so, watching the King, storing up in a moment a lifetime of vertiginous dreams.

He stood a long time on the ledge, holding the cloak, staring down. Did the King live, clutching some ledge?

He called out, his voice a croak. No sound answered. Then, down at the base of the house, the signal light winked again. Whoever was down there had seen nothing, heard nothing.

Would they expect some password, some sign?

No. All they looked for was a little man, dressed in black, alone and unarmed. Little. Dressed in black.

He looked at the greasy rag in his hands, and at the way he must go down, and a dark wave of fear and disgust washed over him.

3

Whenever Caredd the Protector Redhand's wife reined in her horse, the riders in King's livery reined in theirs not far off. The two had some difficulty in keeping with her as closely as their orders required, and out of pity for them she paused often to let them catch up.

It was that luminous harvest day when the world, dying, seems never more alive. A chill wind pressed against her, flushing her cheek like an autumn fruit. Dark, changeful clouds, pierced by sunrays that moved like lamp beams over the colored Downs, hurried elsewhere overhead; when they were gone they left the sky hard, blue, filled up with clean wind to its height.

She rode everywhere over Redsdown from white misty morning to afternoon, overseeing the slow wagons that toiled toward the barns under their great weight of harvest; planning the horse-gathering with the horsemaster as cheerfully as though no war were being waged; stopping everywhere to talk to the children who scared the birds from the grain and the old ones who sat in the year's last sun in their cottage doorways. She was Redsdown's mistress, servant, its reins were in her hands, and yet when she reined in a short way from where the road ran Outward screened by dusty trees, she had a mad impulse to fly to it, outrun her pursuers, make for her husband's tent.

As she stood there, she could hear, coming closer, the sound of wagons and many men. She turned her horse and rode for higher, nearer ground; those two followed.

It was an army that moved Outward, raising dust. Through the screen of trees along the road, she could see the long lances that stood up, bannered and glinting, and the tops of heavy war wagons, and the heads of a glum, endless line of footsoldiers. Boys like her own Redsdown boys, like the two who watched her. She stood in her stirrups and waved to her guards to come close. They were hesitant and, when they did canter up, deferential. They were both very young.

"Whose army is that?"

"The King Red Senlin's Son's, Lady."

"Where do they go?"

"To punish the outlaw Redhand."

"The Protector Redhand," the other said quickly. "And the Queen."

Her horse turned impatiently beneath her, and she steadied him with a gloved hand. In the midst of the line of march she could see a canopy, in the King's colors, moving like a pretty boat along the stream of men.

"Who is that carried in a litter?"

"The King, Lady."

"Taken sick," the other said.

"Will he die?"

"We will all die, Lady."

She thought suddenly of dark Sennred in the tower room: *When I am King . . .*

Around them in the yellow pasture wind threshed the ripened weeds, broadcast seed. Insects leaped at the horse's feet, murmuring. The sky had turned a lapidary green on the horizon, marbled faintly with wisps of cloud. Till it was nearly dark, the columns and wagons and mounted men and pennons went by.

She did not wish the King's death.

She shuddered, violently, with not wishing it. And turned her eager horse homeward.

Homeward.

The last house in the world was a squat tower of wood and stone on the lake's Outward shore. Patches of weed grew close around it as though for shelter, but there was no other life; beyond, the beach, undifferentiated, a rusted color, went on as far as could be seen.

There was no sign of the last man who lived there.

From the tower, a long tongue of pier stuck out over the water. Staying as far from the tower as they could, the birdmen piled up on the pier's end, silently and hurriedly, a large supply of food in oiled skins, and many bundles of sticks wrapped up too. They put off the girl and the Secretary and then rowed as fast as they could away.

Nod and the Secretary stood on the pier, waiting.

"The sticks are for a beacon," the Secretary said. He pointed to the closed door at the pier's end that led into the tower. "He lights it. To warn the birdmen when they come too near the shore."

"Why do they need such a warning?"

"It angers *him*, they said. This one who lives here is called Sop to His Anger."

"How long has he been here?"

"Since Old Fan died, they said. If he lives to be as old as Old Fan, they said, he will have to light the beacon only sixty summers more."

"Horrible."

"He will go mad soon. The madness will give him strength to live. They said it was his gift."

There was a curious wind here, blowing Inward, that they did not remember feeling on the lake. It was steady, insistent, like the gentle pressure of fingers pushing them away. It played within the tower, a penetrating, changeless note.

The door at the end of the pier began to open, squeaking, resisting, as though long unused.

The last man in the world was not a man; he was a boy, skinny as death and as hollow-eyed, with lank black hair down his back and a stain of beard on his white cheeks. He stared at them, hesitant, seeming to want to flee, or speak, or smile, or scream, but he said nothing; only his haunted eyes spoke; they were a beacon, but what they warned of could not be told...

On top of his tower the ashes of the previous night's beacon were still warm.

Since all around them was flat, the tower seemed a giddy height. Nothing anywhere stood up. Inward there was the lake and the sky like it; horizonless, empty, bleeding imperceptibly into night. Outward the featureless beach went on toward the Deep; out there was an occasional vortex of dust. The sun, setting, seemed huge, a distended ball, vaporous and red.

Nod felt poised between nothings, the world divided into two blank halves by the shoreline: the gray, misty half of the lake, and the rust-colored half of desert and dust. The sun frightened her. Almost without meaning to, she slipped her arm into the Secretary's, stood half-sheltered behind him, like a child.

"He'll give us food for a week, ten days. Fuel for the lamp," the Secretary said.

Why a week? Nod thought. How does he know the world will end in a week?

The last man in the world nodded, in assent or at something he saw Outward. The wind lifted his lank black hair, threw strands around his face that now and again he raised a hand to brush away slowly, abstractedly.

"I see his eye out there, sometimes," he said, in a voice thin and sweet as a quickwing's. "I see his eye, like a little moon. I hear him."

"What does he say?" the Secretary asked.

"He says *Silence*," said the last man.

* * *

There is an edge, a lip, Fauconred had said to him on that day in the beginning of his life when they had stood together watching the horse-gathering; *an edge, as on a tray; and then nothing.*

For days the horizon seemed to draw closer, not as though they approached a ridge of mountains but as though the world steadily, imperceptibly foreshortened. When the sun set they could see a dark line at the horizon, a band of shadow that thickened each evening.

Beneath their feet, what had been in the first days recognizably sand changed character, became harder, less various; the occasional rain-cut ravine, even pebbles and earthly detritus, became scarcer. What they walked on was hard, infinitely wearying, like an endless flat deck; it seemed faintly, regularly striated, the striations leading Outward.

Somehow, impossibly, it seemed they came closer to the sun.

Each evening it set in a blank, cloudless sky; vast and shapeless, almost seeming to make a sound as it squatted on the horizon, it threw their shadows out behind them as far as they had come. It lit nothing; there was nothing to reflect it. The earth's faint striations deepened. Like stones across a game board, they rolled toward their Player.

Then on a night the setting sun lit something.

At the top of the band of shadow that was the world's edge something caught the sun's fire for a moment, lit up with its light, a spark only, and it faded quickly. If there had been anything, anything else to see in all that vastness, he would not have noticed its brief light.

"Look," he said, and she stopped. She would not raise her eyes; she could no longer bear the setting sun. When she did look up, the sign was gone. He could only tell her it had been there; she only looked from him to the fast-darkening edge whose shadow swept toward them; expressionless, faceless almost, like a brutalized child.

How was it, that as far Outward as she had gone, just so far within had she gone also? With every step a layer of her seemed to come away; something she had been as sure of as her name became tenuous, then untenable, and was shed like skin. She had not known how many of these layers she owned, how many she had to lose. When she felt she had been bared utterly, was naked as a needle of all notions, suppositions, wants, needs, she found there was more that the silence and emptiness could strip her of.

She had never hated him. Whatever in her could have hated him had been rubbed off, far away, on the cliffs of the Edge maybe. Now he was the only other in the world, and she found that the needle of being left her by solitude needed him utterly, beyond speaking, for they had spoken little lately; only there had come a day she could not go on unless he held her hand, and a night when she would not stop weeping unless he held her, held her tight.

So they had gone on, hand in hand.

They raised the shelter, there where he had seen the sign, though it was neither hot nor cold there. Partly they sought protection from the wind, which was not strong, only insistent and unceasing, like hopelessness; mostly, though, when it was pitched, they had a place amid placelessness.

They had not imagined, on the soundless lake, to what an unbearable pitch soundlessness could be tuned.

"What do you love?" she sobbed, muffled in his red robe late at night, curled within his arms. "What do you love? Tell me. What means more than love to you? What makes you laugh? What would you die for?" Her tears wet his chest, tears warmer than his flesh. He couldn't answer; he only rocked her in rhythm with her fast-beating heart, till she was quieter.

"What will you do," she asked then, "when you find him?"

"Ask him why he has summoned me."

"And what will he answer?"

Silence.

When the sun next day was overhead and they had no shadow, they came on the first step.

The step was low, cut sharp as though with tools, and it was wide, seemed to go on around the world, and it was so deep they could not see if it led to another. They stopped a moment, because it was a marker, and there had been no other all day. She tightened her grip on his hand and they stepped upward. Far, far behind a bird screamed, so startling they both jumped as though their stepping up had caused it; they looked back but could see no bird.

The next step when they came to it was perceptibly higher; beyond, closer, they could see the next, higher still.

Through the afternoon they climbed toward the top of the edge of the world, which lay above and ahead seeming sharp and flat as a blade. The steps grew shallower and higher in a geometric progression, each seeming to double the last, until toward sunset the steps they climbed were higher than they were deep, and the edge of the world was perpendicular above them. They were in its shadow.

Along the stair that circled the world there were huge flaws in its perfection: it seemed to slow the heart to imagine the shudderings of earth needed to crack and split that geometry, reduce its plated, flawless surface to glittering rubble. At an ungraspable distance away a pitted stone, a moon perhaps, something vast, had imbedded itself in the stair, blasting its levels for great distances. It was terrifying in its congruity, the unfathomable stair, the unfathomable stone.

It was they who were incongruous.

He was above her on the climb; sat on the stair

holding his hand down to her to pull her up with him. Both wore the rags of the clothes they had left Forgetful in, his red domino, her hooded cloak, climbing steps never meant for anything like them; flesh in that desert.

The last step was a ledge barely wide enough to stand on and a sheer wall taller by far than he. He inched along it sidewise, she below him on the next stair, until they were nearer the catastrophic damage. There they struggled up through a broken place, their hands and knees bleeding from the malevolent surfaces, until he dragged himself groaning over the last ledge and came out onto the last place in the world. He turned, trembling, and drew her up with him.

It was nothing but the top of the last step. It was wide, but they could see the edge of it, jagged, more broken than the stair. And beyond that nothing, nothing, nothing at all. A veil of cloud extended Outward from the edge like a ledge of false earth, and the sun stained it brown and orange; but through the veil they could see that the Nothing went down, down, thickening into darkness.

There were two things there with them at the edge. There was the wind, stronger, filled with a presence they could not face into, though they had sought it so long. And there was, not far from where they came up, an egg of some soft silver, as high as a man, seamless, fired with sunset light.

He had never been sure, not for a moment, that he had been right, that he had saved from his damaged knowledge the right clues, the right voice. Not till now.

He went to it, touched the hand that was a reflection of his own hand in the glassy surface. Turned to look back to Nod: she crouched on the shelf of the world, touching its surface with her hands, as though afraid she might fall off.

"That," she said, and another would not have heard her tiny voice.

"A . . . Vehicle." He went to sit with her.

They watched the sunset fire fade from it in silence.

"What will you do?" she said at last.

"Eat," he said, and took from his pack a little of the food that the Last Man had given them, broke it and gave her some.

The egg turned ghostly blue in the evening, then dark, seemed to disappear. She threaded her thin arm in his which was cold as steel, colder than ever.

"If you must return alone," he said.

"No."

"If you must..."

"No."

He said nothing further. It grew cold and she began to shiver, but stopped then as through an effort of will.

In the night, it was almost possible to believe they were not where they were. The stars, cold, distant, seemed familiar and near.

She felt him suddenly tense beside her, could almost feel the workings of his senses.

"*Yes,*" he said, and the wind snatched away his word. The wind rose.

He went to the egg, touched the stars that seemed to cover its surface. The wind rose.

The wind rose, invaded him, filled him as though he were hollow, made him deaf then blind, then utterly insensate: calm in silence. The Blindness compressed itself into a voice, or the metaphor of a voice, speaking to senses he had not known he had; lovely, wise, murmurous with sleep.

You have come late, Recorder.

His being strove to speak, but he could find no voice.

Go, then, said his Blindness. *Go to him, he awaits you.*

Leviathan, he tried to say, *Leviathan.*

Blindness trembled, as though unsure, and withdrew in a roar of silence. The last place in the world congealed before the Recorder's eyes, like the false place of a dream though he had never dreamt, and he saw Nod on her knees, mouth open, an idiot's face.

He cried out, not knowing what he said, desperate that Blindness might not return. He pressed his naked cheek against the cold egg and waited. Waited...

Blindness, angry, inchoate, whipped through him.

Why are you not gone?

Now he found the voice to speak to that Voice: I know no way to go, he said. Do I trouble you?

Yes.

Only tell me then what I must do.

How am I to know if you do not? it asked.

You don't know?

Not what task he might have set you other than to Record, for which you were made, and could not but do.

It wasn't you...?

I?

You who made me, you who summoned me.

Summoned, perhaps. Guided, as a beacon. But not made. No. What would I want with your Recording? I have forgotten more than he has ever created. It is my skill.

Who is he, then? Is he Leviathan?

I am Leviathan; so men call me. He is...other than me. A brother.

Where is he? How am I to come to him?

Where now? I cannot tell. Your Vehicle will find him. A journey of a thousand years. More. Less...Only go. Open that Vehicle. You have the key, not I.

I have no key, said the Recorder to his Blindness, feeling withered by an awful impatience pressing him to go: I have no key, Leviathan, I am damaged, I have forgotten everything; help me. Help me.

Help. I cannot...

Begin at the beginning, the Recorder said; and, as he had to the two Endwives on the Drum: perhaps something will return to me, some part of the way I am made, that will tell me what to do.

Beginnings, said Blindness. *You don't know what you ask. I have forgotten beginnings of worlds that were dead before this one was born.*

The Recorder heard no more then; but he waited, for he seemed to feel deep stirrings, a Thought drawn up painfully from some ancient gulf. *I have forgotten*, Blindness began again at last, *forgotten how it was I came here . . . But it was I who dropped the pillar into the placeless deeps . . . I who set this roof, to protect me from the heaven stones.*

You made the world.

My house this world; my roof, holding place, shelter. Beneath it I lived, down deep where it is hot and dense and changeless. I was alone. Then he brought them.

Men.

It was mine before they came. It will be mine when they are gone.

How did he bring them?

Sailed.

How, sailed . . .

He has sails, and I do not. We are not alike. He is busy and wide-ranging; I am sleepy and stationary. He has sails; sails like woven air, that fine; large as the world. Many of them. They are his speed.

Spread sails to catch the Light of Suns . . .

Yes, he did so. Bringing them.

From where?

Elsewhere. What could it matter? A journey of a thousand years. Less. More.

How did they survive?

He did not bring living men; no, they are too fragile for that; he brought instead a sliver of each, a grain, a seed, from which he could grow a whole man when he chose. These seeds or what you will could make the journey, though the men could not . . .

There were fifty-two.

Perhaps. And all their grasses, the green things proper to them, and their beasts too, one of each—no, two, one of each sex. And he set out each in turn to grow on my naked roof: increase and multiply. And set out the men last, new-grown.

And then.

And looked on it all, and saw that it was good.

The Recorder was desperate to pause, to assemble all this, to let it combine within him and form some answer; but Leviathan trembled at his hesitation. Wait, he said then; I have understood nothing; tell me who I am, what is to become of me; why he made me.

He does not trust me.

Not trust you...

I owed him a service, from another time. He put them in my charge. I have watched as well as I could, between sleepings. When he has not trusted me, he has had you.

Me?

You and others like you; recorders, adjusters. He has not forgotten. It is his chiefest toy, this world; no, not chiefest, not any longer. But he has not forgotten. And when he wishes to have senses here, he casts a recorder among men. A thing, his invention, his finger.

Why?

It must be kept in balance. That is the play, the whole jest. It is a small world, Recorder; my back only; it must be pruned, regulated. So there have been adjusters: warmakers, peacemakers, idiots, cardplayers. His invention is endless.

The Just.

The Just. A fine adjustment. The smaller wheel that justifies the large. He fashioned a Notion for them, you see; and when they gathered round it, he put the pruning knife into their hands. The Gun I mean. And so the thing is kept in balance ...

The Recorder's utter attention had shifted, minutely:
Nod . . .

Who is there with you?

She brought me.

Brought you?

I didn't know the Task, or how to come to you to ask
what it was. She led me.

*It doesn't matter. She cannot hear. Deaf. Deaf, blind,
dumb; as they all are.*

As I am.

*Well. You are a thing of his. He will know if there is
any use left in you.*

I think . . . I will not go to him.

Recorder.

Why? Why did men agree to such a thing?

They asked it.

They could not have.

*That is the tale, Recorder. He came to them on his
endless, busy way; he found them on the last undesolated
shelf of some wretched ruined stone. They worshiped
him; that has always been his pleasure. He granted
their desire.*

What was their desire?

*An end to Change. What other desire is there?
"Take us away," they prayed, "to a new world, like the
one our ancientest ancestors lived in, a small world
where the sun rises and hastens to the place where he
arose, where we can live forever and where nothing
runs away." So I remember him telling it . . .*

And he brought them here. Here.

*They didn't know themselves. They made a bad
bargain. We kept our part.*

Did you?

*They wanted eternal life; he gave them perpetual
motion. It comes to the same thing, for such a race.*

Why? What did he gain?

I don't remember. Some satisfaction. It had nothing

to do with me. For the amusement of it only, perhaps, probably . . .

Does he know how men suffer?

Do they suffer?

I think, the Recorder said, I think I do not choose to return to him.

You think. You do not choose. Recorder! He has expended energy on your creation. He will not see it wasted. He wastes nothing. Every part of you is minutely inscribed; he will disentangle you utterly, leach from your every thread what it is dyed with. He looks forward to it.

I think I . . .

Recorder! I awoke from sleep to welcome you, awoke from depths and lengths of sleep you cannot imagine. Speaking to your ignorance is anguish. Go to him. If you can speak, then, ask him to illuminate you; if you can speak, perhaps he will answer you . . .

Unable to bear more, the Recorder sought within him for some barrier to hide from that lovely Voice behind, some refusal, some power . . . He found it. It would rise within him if he could find the strength to summon it: he found strength: it rose, blocking the blind madness.

As though far off, but coming closer, the last place in the world began to appear to him. And the nature of the wall he had found became clear:

He was screaming.

All his multiple strengths drew to his throat, drew in to be pressed into sound, a long, breathless, continual sound that grew louder as it rose higher until it ceased to be sound. The sound searched him, cleansed him, healed him, broke into places within him sealed since the Gun, and let out all his wounded knowledge.

With horror he remembered all. Who he was. What had made him. And why: he knew the whole Plot he had been made for, the reason for his hideous strength,

the blood-hero he was to have been, the long war that
would never happen now . . .

And with the great knowledges came a small one: he
knew why it was he screamed, for at a certain pitch and
loudness the egg before him opened soundlessly.

His scream had opened his Vehicle. It was the key.

He ceased; the sound lingered, ran away, died; he
stood with his wide chest throbbing, done.

It was near dawn. Inward the stars faded in an
empurpled sky. Nod lay before him, prostrate, hands
against her ears, her face pressed against the ground.
When the sound was gone she lifted her head, her
tear-streaked face, looked at him, couldn't look away.

The wind had risen, pitiless, like no wind of the
world. It tore at his ragged robe, urging him to discard
it. He kicked off his cracked boots. He drew out the
Gun, dropped it; undid his belt and let the garment go.
It stepped away on the wind for a moment as though
possessed, and then collapsed.

The wind could not touch him then. His skin shone,
impervious, seamed with bright silver threads, knotted
with weird muscle. Hairless, sexless, birthless, deathless.

"Neither-nor," Nod breathed, seeing him thus.
"Neither-nor."

There was a part of himself, he knew now, that he
had invented; had had to invent because of the damage
done him. There was a Truth that his invention had
allowed him to discover, that he was not meant or made
to discover. That invented part wanted him to take up
the girl, hold her as he seemed to remember he once
had, speak comfort to her. That invented part, which
his Maker could not have foreseen, wanted . . . it wanted.

He lifted Nod to her knees.

"Well, I will speak to him," he said, his hoarse voice
nearly wind-lost. "I promise. Speak to him, ask him . . ."

"No!" she said. "Stay!"

He turned from her; that invented part was fading,
disengaging; it was unnecessary now that he was whole

again. Yet he would save one question. One question, over the whole length of his huge journey. He went to the open Vehicle, found a way to fit himself within it.

"No! you said *no* . . ."

The wind turned around, sucked suddenly into the Deep. It screamed as it ran down, bellowed, sobbed, shrieked. The ledge of earth trembled. As silently as it had opened, the Vehicle closed, closing the Recorder within it.

Nod, sobbing, unable to stand, searched for Suddenly on hands and knees; the wind, tortured, turned again and fled upward. The Vehicle began slowly to spin on its axis.

The Vehicle rose into the air, spinning faster.

And Leviathan arose from the Deep to bid his brother's thing farewell.

Mad, Nod ran toward the edge, toward the hugeness that rose from the Deep, screaming, screaming obscenities, pleading, reviling. As it rose it eclipsed each wavering star beyond; when it was so high it blotted out all the sky above her and looked, she thought, down toward her with an eye larger than night, she fired Suddenly toward the eye, trying to fling all of herself along the barrel with the little ball against that hatefulness.

For she had heard. Heard it all, all. She fell with the shock of the explosion; fell where his garment had come to rest on the ledge of earth; she clutched its worn stuff and knew nothing for a time.

But she had heard, and had recorded.

4

They would say of the King Red Senlin's Son in later times that he was the tallest, the handsomest man of his age; that anyone who ever saw him in armor never forgot the splendor.

They would date an age's beginning from his reign, and cherish the glories of his new City, the wit of his poets, the loveliness of his artisans' work. They would forget his arrogance, his indulgence, his spendthrift luxury, and why should they not? They would remember only that he was handsome, and that his love was great, and that his reign was brief.

The tale told children would relate how with his architects he had worked in rain and by torchlight on the great Harran Stone and caught a fatal chill. It would not mention the traitor-god Blem, or the leaves called Sleep that he inhaled, or the violence of his lovers against him. It made no difference. Beneath the Stone he slept awhile and was no more; nor Harrah either. The Stone remained.

They woke him from a thick, feverish sleep, men masked in armor, whom he at first did not recognize.

"They are a mile out on the Drum," said one, his voice muffled by steel.

"Fifty watchfires. Stronger than we thought."

The King stared at them, sitting on the edge of his bed. "Redhand."

They looked one to another.

"This is all his work," the King said dully. "His crime."

They said nothing for a moment. Then: "The Queen is there too," one said.

He only looked at them. There were waves of familiar, enervating pain in him, and his limbs were cold. What had they said? "Bring me the drawings."

"Will you ride out?" one of them said. "See them there, see your army?"

"It would do them good to see you armed," the other said.

"Bring me the drawings," the King said. "Where is my brother?"

They surrendered then; one of them brought to him a wide, shallow wooden case stained with ink. The other stood at the tent door a moment, slapping one heavy glove into the other gloved hand, then turned and left.

The King fumbled with the lock, got it open; he turned up the lamp and spread out the drawings of the Harran Stone.

It was all there, from the first crude imagining in smudged charcoal to the final details of every carved figure cross-hatched in pale brown ink. He would never cease wondering at its calm, perfect volumes, its changeful expression of grief, strength, pride, quiet, solitude. How had they achieved it, through what magic? Behind it some of the drawings showed the old rotunda, a deadweight, gross, pig-eyed, with the chaotic towers of a thousand reigns bristling on its backside.

That must come down. He would see to it.

Down in the heart of that poised monument, down where every line drew the eye and every finger pointed, lay the Stone that covered Black Harrah. And here were drawn the carvings that covered that stone.

But how, the King thought for the thousandth time, how will he breathe there, beneath the stone? He felt his own breath constricted. "Redhand," he said again. He turned to the armed presence he felt hovering behind him. "Bring me my armor..."

He was alone in the tent.

He turned back slowly to the drawings, the thought of Redhand already leaking away from him. He turned the crackling, yellow sheets.

Down in the corner of a drawing that showed a mechanism for lifting stones, the architect had made another little sketch, a strange thing, something that had nothing to do with stones, it seemed. There was a diminutive figure, a man, strapped into a device of gears and pedals. Radiating out from the center of the

device, made of struts and fabric, were the wings of a
bird. A bird the size of a man.

For a long time the King stared at it. It would
disappear in a cloud of pain and then appear again, still
in its impossible flight.

How large is the world? the King thought, tracing
the manwings with a trembling finger. How high up is
the sky?

From the windows of his locked carriage the Arbiter
could look out either side at the army that toiled
Inward, gathering strength, through days that darkened
toward winter.

It was not like one beast, as he had often thought an
army would be, marching in time and with fierce
purpose. No, men only; some hung back, contingents
were lost, there were deserters and quarrels daily—
especially in this army of new, uneasy allies. The whole
parade was slung over a mile of Drumskin in an order
that perhaps the captains understood, though he doubted
it.

On a windy, cloud-striated day his carriage was stopped
longer than usual in a stretch of country more desolate
than usual. Perhaps another carriage had lost a wheel
ahead; perhaps his brother and the Queen had had a
falling-out . . .

Toward evening, a cheerless Barnolsweek evening,
Fauconred came to his tent, unlocked its locks with
some embarrassment.

"How is your war?" Learned asked.

"Not long now, Learned," Fauconred said gruffly.
"We take up our positions here."

"And . . ."

"Wait for the King. It will not be long."

"Uncle," Learned said (and Fauconred lowered his
eyes, though Redhand children had always called him
that), "Uncle, will you give this to Redhand?" It was a
folded paper, sealed with his ring.

"Is this . . ." Fauconred began, turning it in his hands.

"No. Only a task I could do, a will. Witness him signing it, and have it sent to Inviolable with this message." He gave Fauconred another paper. Fauconred looked doubtful, and Learned took his old hand. "I won't betray you. I can't help, but I won't betray."

Fauconred looked at him for a moment as though seeking something, some word that would extricate them all from this; not finding it, he tapped the papers against his hand and turned away.

Learned watched him go, solid as a keg, and wondered if he would, in his leather heart, rather win or lose against the King.

On Barnolsweek Eve the King Red Senlin's Son's battle came out of the Downs.

Learned Redhand, allowed to walk a ridge above the Queen's army within sight of a guard, watched as through the day they arranged themselves there, a thousand strong, perhaps more. Tents were raised and banners raised above them, some the same banners that flew above the tents of Redhand's army. Families had been divided; the warriors of the King's father stood against the King; the sons of those who had fought Red Senlin stood beside his son.

He did not see the Son. He saw a royal tent pitched and no one enter it; no banner was raised above it. When it was pitched, Redhand and the Queen came out to see, but no one came forth, and they retired to their separate tents. Learned wondered why they did not mass their army suddenly, and like some swift dagger stab into the King's army while it was in chaos. It was what he would have done. They intended to wait, apparently, like boxers, like the players of a game, wait for their opponents to settle themselves and the contest to begin. Odd . . .

At evening, from his vantage, he saw something that no one else seemed to notice. Off beyond the King's left wing, taking advantage of any cover, any patch of desiccated bush or rain-cut ravine, a young man made his way across the distance of gray heath that separated the two armies. Learned watched him, losing sight of him off and on, and looking away too so that no one would see what he looked at: he did not know this one's business, and like an Endwife wanted not to. He had made his last moves in this quarrel; in the silence of his confinement he had made his farewells to his brothers, had done what he had not before truly done: divested himself of his family. Like a trapped animal, he had escaped by gnawing away a part of himself. He had nothing further to do; but he watched this creeping one till clouded darkness cut him off, and wondered: what if all the noise and clamor and great numbers were so much show, and this one held the game, and, like the single shot of a Gun, could resolve it?

When Redhand later found this boy hidden in the shadows of his tent, dark-hooded, his face smeared with ashes, he made a motion to call guards; but the boy laid a finger on his lips, and gave Redhand a folded paper.

There is a peat-cutter's house, the paper said, *less than five miles from us, along the edge of the Downs, on this side of a bog called Dreaded, by where the Harran Road comes out. On the night after you have this, come there. Come alone, or send only one other ahead to assure yourself there is no danger. Tell no one, most especially the Queen. I will be there, alone. I swear by our friendship no harm will come to you; I trust our friendship none will come to me. Redhand, there is much you should know that you do not.*

Sennred

"This is lies," Redhand said, folding it carefully.

The boy said nothing.

"Sennred is prisoner in the City."

"I don't know his face," the boy said. "Only that he who gave that to me was a little man, dark, and one of

his shoulders was higher than the other. And he said he
was Sennred."

"Did he tell you," Redhand said, "that you will be
hanged, and cut apart, and your body strewn before
your army, to answer this?"

The boy said nothing.

"Why you? How were you chosen? Are you a man of
Sennred's that he chose you?"

"I'm . . . no one. They asked for a volunteer. I chose
myself."

"Whose household are you?"

"I come from Fennsdown."

Redhand read the letter again and fed it thoughtfully
to the brazier. "How will you return? Have you thought
of that?"

"I will not. Only allow me to escape, and I will go
Outward. There are no sentries there."

"And what will he tell me in this house?"

"I can't read," the boy said. "I don't know what's
written there."

An ash of the letter rose from the brazier and settled
again like a bird. "Step back," Redhand said, striking
the gong beside him, "back behind the curtains there."

A red-jacketed man entered as the boy hid himself.
"Go to the Defender Fauconred," Redhand said.
"Send him to me." The guard turned to go. "Listen.
Speak only to Fauconred. Tell him to come when the
watch changes. Tell no one else."

When they were alone again, the boy came from
behind the curtain. He had pulled back his hood to
show short, blond hair and fair skin above the ashes
smeared on his face.

"The watch will be changing," Redhand said. "Go
now."

Unhooded, the boy reminded him of someone; he
could not remember who, nor in what scene in his life;
perhaps in a dream only. "You're brave," he said. "Will
they reward you?"

The war-viols of the water sounded. The boy hooded himself, turned into the shadows, lifted the edge of Redhand's tent and was gone.

In armor but without weapons, wrapped to their eyes in dark cloaks that blew as their horses' manes and tails blew, Fauconred and Redhand looked down at evening from a swell of Drumskin onto a thick-set peat-cutter's hovel. Dull light spilled from its single window into the little yard; its gate swung in the wind.

Fauconred pulled the cloak from around his mouth. "I'll go down."

Redhand looked behind him the way they had come; no one had followed.

"Wait here," Fauconred said. "Wait till I signal." He spurred his horse into a gentle trot and rode carefully down on the hut. At the yard he dismounted, led his horse around the turn of the wall out of sight.

Redhand's horse stamped, and the clash of his trappings was loud in the stillness.

The great gray heath, patent though glum by day, had grown moody and secretive as evening came on. There were glimmers and ripples of light somewhere at the edge of vision, that were not there when Redhand turned to look at them; evening light only, perhaps, changeful in the wind-combed grass... There were pockets of dark that bred fogs like dim slow beasts; there was the bog, Dreaded, prostrate beyond the little house; out there rotting things lit hooded candles that moved like conspirators, moved on him...

No. He was alone, utterly alone. For a moment he could even believe he was the only man alive anywhere.

Fauconred finished his inspection, came around the house and waved to him. As Redhand approached him, a cloaked ghost in the last light wary by the low door, he thought: what if he... in league with them... His hair stood on end. The idiot notion passed almost as it was born, but Redhand felt himself trembling faintly as he dismounted.

"No one," Fauconred said. "No one here but the Folk."

"Watch," Redhand said; he gave his reins to Fauconred and stooped to enter the little round doorway.

Two women cowled in shawls sat by a peat fire; they looked up when he entered, their faces minted into bright coins by the firelight. "Protector," said one, and they looked away. There was a movement in the house's only other room; Redhand turned, the wide boards of the floor cried out faintly; he could see someone, sick or asleep, in a loft in that room.

"Do you have a lamp?" he asked.

"There's the fire," the younger woman said. And the other quoted: "There's no lamp the foolish can see better by."

He sat then, in an old reed chair that groaned familiarly. Everything here spoke, the wind, twisted by a crack at the window, cried out in a little voice, the sleeping one stirred, sighed, the women sang: If Barnol wets the Drum with rain, then Caermon brings the Downs the same; if Caermon wets the Downs with rain, the Hub will not be dry till Fain brings the New Year round again; new year old year still the same . . .

At first Redhand started at every noise; but then the fire began to melt the chill of the Drum from him, and loosen too something tight that had held him. He sighed, inhaling the dark odor of the cottage.

There was a sentiment, among court poets, that this little life, cottage life, was the only true and happy one; filled up with small cares but without real burdens, and rich with the immortality of changelessness. Redhand had never felt so, had never envied the poor, surely not the peat-cutters and cottagers. No, there were no young people here, and Redhand knew why—they had escaped, probably to take up some untenanted farm, glad enough to get a piece of land, a share of the world, and to see their children then buy or inherit more, become owners, and their grandchildren perhaps Defenders, and so on and on till the descendants of these women singing the seasons entered the topmost spiral of the world and were flung Outward into pride, and war, and the Guns.

Two parents, Learned had said, four grandparents, eight great-grandparents, sixteen great-great-grand-parents, thirty-two, sixty-four, one hundred and twenty-eight . . . We three, he had said, are part of it. Redhand, Learned, Younger.

Brothers. Well, that was easy, then; not every man needed all those ancestors, he shared them with others. Was that the solution? It wasn't sufficient; still the number of ancestors must be multiplied as you stepped back through the generations, how many thousands of them, each doubling the last, till the vast population needed to begin the world spilled over its edges into the Deep. It was mad . . .

It came to him as a sounding clarity, a benign under-standing that made the close cottage order itself before his eyes and smile.

All those millions were dead; and when the Fifty-two began the world, the millions weren't yet born.

Yes, their shades crowded the edges of the world; yes, there were uncountable numbers of them. But they weren't alive, had never been alive all at once; they were simply all the people that had ever been, added up as though a farmer were to reckon his harvest by counting all the grain from all the seed he had ever sowed. Absurd that he could have been tricked into thinking that they needed all to live at once. Gratefully, the world closed up within him to a little place, a place of few; a handful at a time, who must give way to those who would come after.

Give way . . .

The structure of the burning peat was like a thousand tiny cities in flames. It held him; he watched ramparts crumble, towers fall, maddened populaces. Hung above the fire was a fat black kettle he hadn't noticed before. It had begun to boil; thick coils of steam rose from it. Now and again, the younger of the women took from within her clothes a handful of something, seeds or spices, and threw them in. The pot boiled more furiously each time she did so, frothing to its edges. The old one was anxious, cried out each time the pot began to seethe.

"Protector," she said, "help us here, or the pot will overflow."

"Why does she do that?" Redhand asked. "Let it subside."

"I must, I must," the younger said, and threw in more; a trickle of the froth this time ran over the kettle's edge and sizzled with an acrid odor. The old one gasped as though in pain. "Protector," she said, "remember your vows. Help the Folk."

He got up, not certain what he must do. Within the kettle a mass of stuff seethed and roiled; the younger woman flung in her seed, the stuff rose as though in helpless rage. Calmly then, with their eyes on him, he bent his head to the kettle to drink the boiling excess.

He started awake.

There was a horse in the courtyard. A man was dismounting. Fauconred threw open the door. "Sennred," he said. "Alone."

There was no kettle . . . The two women hurried away timidly into the other room when Sennred came in. His face, never youthful, looked old in the firelight. "I would have come sooner," he said, "only I wanted not to be followed." He held out his hand to Redhand, who hesitated, still addled with his dream. He got up slowly and took Sennred's hand.

"Does the King," he said, "know of this meeting?"

Almost imperceptibly, Sennred shook his head.

"Has he forgiven you?"

"I hope he has."

"He released you from prison."

"I broke from prison." He undid the cloak he wore, let it fall. He touched Redhand, gently, to pass by him, and sat heavily in the single chair. "I broke from prison with Little Black."

"With him?"

"He showed me the way out. We became... great friends in prison." A faint smile faded quickly; he cradled his pale forehead in his hand and went on, not looking at Redhand. "We climbed to the roof of our prison. And then down. At a certain point... at a certain point, Black fell..."

"Lies." With a sudden fierce anger, Redhand saw the story. "Lies."

"I grasped his cloak as he fell," Sennred went on, in the same tone, as though he hadn't been interrupted. "But the cloak wouldn't hold. He fell. I saw it."

"Who wrote this tale?" Redhand growled. "One of the King's urnings? And did you practice it then?"

"Redhand..."

"No. Sennred. It's a poor trick." But his neck thrilled; Sennred's look was steady, with an eerie tenderness; he didn't go on—it seemed inconsequential to him whether Redhand believed him or not. "Why," Redhand said, and swallowed, "why is the King not here then? Why is this done in secret? Shout it out to my army, to the Queen..."

"No. The Blacks would think their King was murdered..."

"Was he not?"

"They would fight. Redhand. Listen to me now. I want to begin with no war. This was never my quarrel. The King said to me: *burn Redhand's house, his fields; let nothing live*. I won't. It hurts me, Redhand, not to do what he asked. But I can't."

"What are you saying?"

"I'm asking you to desert the Queen. Take your army away. Decamp, by night. There will be no reprisals. I swear it."

A weird apprehension rose in Redhand's throat like spittle. "And who are you?" he said, almost whispered. "Who are you, Sennred, to swear such a thing?"

"Heir. Heir to it all: Black and Red. There's no other. Redhand, the King Red Senlin's son is dead."

With a sudden whirr all Redhand's tense suspicions, doubts, plans took flight, left him for a moment blindly empty. Why had he not realized . . . ? With sickening certainty, he knew he was about to weep.

Give way, give way . . .

Toward dawn, Sennred rode away. Fauconred handed him up, and he and Redhand watched till he was gone.

"Go on, then," Redhand said. "We shouldn't return together."

"No." The old man mounted with clumsy grace and pulled his cloak around him. "The sun won't shine today."

"No. Fog, I think. A Drumskin fog."

"It will be easier then."

"Yes. Go now."

Fauconred stood his horse a moment; a cock crowed. He thought he knew what it was his cousin felt, but knew nothing to say to it. He saluted, and spurred his heavy horse.

Redhand stood a long time in the little yard, watching the air thicken around him. It was utterly still. A red dawn Inward was being extinguished as fast as it grew; Dreaded was thick with fog.

What if he was wrong?

All those boys and men, their loins rich with descendants, would escape death tomorrow. Perhaps it was wrong that they should live, perhaps their children's children, that might not be, would boil over the edges of the little world . . . He shrugged it all away. The truth he had glimpsed had grown tenuous and thin; he vowed not to touch it again. He was not one for notions; he was only grateful for what he felt now: calm, peaceful almost, for the first time in many weeks.

Behind him, sudden in the stillness, the shutters of

the cottage banged shut. He turned, saw a frightened face look out before the last one closed. When he turned back, someone was coming toward him, out of the fog, from Dreaded.

As the figure condensed out of the whiteness, he saw with a rush of joy that it was his lost Secretary, of whom he had not thought in weeks. But then, no, the figure came closer, changed; it wasn't him.

It was the blond boy who had brought him Sennred's message.

Redhand stepped toward him, was about to speak to him, tell him what had come of his mission. Then he saw the Gun in the boy's hands.

They stood for a moment not far apart.

The boy's only thought was a hope that the old Gun not misfire in the wet. Redhand felt only a faint resentment that the boy had told him he couldn't read.

The shot made Fauconred's horse start, and Fauconred cry out. It echoed long, rolling through the low country, almost reaching the place of two armies before the fog drowned it at last.

There were two Endwives, a young girl named Norin, an old woman named Ser, who had come several miles through the fog with a hospital wagon, not sure of the way, getting down now and again to lead the horses, who were afraid to go on; sure then that they had lost the way in the fog. Toward night, though, which was a thickening of the fog only, they came to high ground. There were lights, watchfires, dull gobbets of flame in the wetness: their sisters.

Through the night, others arrived, fog-delayed; they prepared themselves, listening to the faint sounds of a multitude on the plain below them, moving, stirring— arming themselves, probably. They talked little, saying only what was necessary to their craft; hoping, without speaking it, that the fog would hold, and there would be no battle.

Before dawn, a wind came up. They could feel it cold on their Outward cheeks; it began to tear at the fog. Their watchfires brightened; as day came on, their wagons assembled there began to appear to them, gradually clearer, as though they awoke from a drug.

When the sun rose the fog was in flight. Long bars of sunlight fell across the plain where the battle was to be.

But there was no battle there.

There was one army of men, vast, chaotic, the largest army anyone had ever seen. There was a royal tent in its center, and a Dog banner above it; and there was a flag near it that bore a red palm. It was quiet; no war viols played; the Endwives thought they could hear faint laughter.

Opposite, where the other army should have been, there were a hundred guttering campfires. There were some tents of black, half dismantled. Soldiers, too, scattered contingents late in realizing what had happened in the night, but not many; the many were away over the Drum, a long raggedy crowd, no army, going Outward, not having planned on it, quickly.

By noon there was no one at all facing the world's largest army. All who had not joined it had fled it.

Only a single closed carriage remained. Beside it, a man in a wide black hat stood with his hands behind his back, the freshening breeze teasing the hem of his black coat. The carriage's dappled gelding quietly cropped the sparkling, sunlit grass.

EPILOGUE

When the snows came, the Neither-nor hibernated.

Deep in a rug-hung cave, in a bed piled with covers, pillows, furs, It dozed through week on week of storm that stifled Its forest, locked the Door.

In Rathsweek, pale and weak as an invalid, the Neither-nor crept out from bed, to the cave-mouth, to look out. The forest glinted, dripped, sparkled with melting snow; the rock walls of the glen were ruined ice palaces where they were not nude and black.

It was a day, by Its reckoning, sacred to Rizna, a day when Birth stirs faintly below the frost, deep in the womb of Death. Not a day to look out, alone, on a winter forest, spy on its nakedness. But the Neither-nor was not afraid of powers; It owned too many for that; and when the figure in red appeared far off, like blood on the snow, the Neither-nor awaited it calmly, shivering only in the cold.

But when it came close, stumbling, knee-deep in snow, near enough to be recognized, the Neither-nor gasped. "I thought you were dead."

The girl's eyes stared, but didn't seem to see. Except for the shivers that racked her awful thinness, and the raggedy red cloak, real enough, the Neither-nor might have still thought her dead.

On feet bound in rags, Nod struggled toward It.
Overcome with pity, the Neither-nor began to make Its
way toward her, but Nod held up an arm; she would
come alone.

When she stood before the Neither-nor she drew out
Suddenly, and with all the little strength left her, struck
the Gun against the rock wall, cracking its stock. "No,"
the Neither-nor said, taking Nod's shoulders in the Two
Hands. "You haven't failed. You haven't. The task is
done. Redhand is dead."

She stood, the broken Gun in her hands, a negation
frozen on her dirty face, and the Neither-nor released
her, frightened, of what It could not tell. And Nod
began to speak.

He had not his brother's enthusiasm for works and
words, but he had loved his brother, deeply, and in his
kingship the works would go forward. In that winter the
Harran Stone was completed; there his brother lay,
with Harrah, their flawed love made so perfect in their
tomb that even in the darkest of winter days, shut up in
the Citadel, Sennred had not sensed his brother's ghost
was restless.

He had turned an old prison into a theater. A scheme
for making books without writing them out by hand,
that Sennred little understood or cared about, he had
fostered anyway.

He looked after these things, and his peace, patiently
through the winter of his mourning. And hers.

It had been easy to confirm her in sole possession, in
perpetuity, of Redsdown; he had with pleasure expunged
every lien, attachment, attainder on the old fortress and
its green hills. To console her further was impossible,
he knew; with grownup wisdom he had let time do
that.

When spring, though, with agonizing delays began to
creep forth, he sent gifts, letters impeccably proper, so
tight-reined she laughed to read them.

And on a day when even in the cold old Citadel perfumey breaths of a shouting spring day outside wandered lost, he prepared to go himself.

There were seven windows in the chamber he sat in. Against six of them the towers of the castle and the City heights held up hands to block the light. The seventh, though, looked out across the lake and the mountains; its broad sill was warm where he laid his hand.

Out there, in those greening mountains, somewhere, the Woman in Red held her councils.

She was not Just, they said, though like the Just she spoke of the old gods—but when she spoke she cursed them. What else she spoke of the King couldn't tell; his informants were contradictory, their abstracts bizarre. Of the woman herself they said only that she wore always a ragged red domino, and that she was a waterman's daughter with cropped blond hair. The Grays thought her dangerous; the old ones' eyes narrowed as they glossed for him one or another fragment of her thought. The King said nothing.

People were stirred, in motion, that was certain. He gathered she spoke to all classes—Just, Defenders, Folk. Some he sent to hear her strange tale listened—and didn't return.

A spring madness. Well, he knew about that...almost, it seemed, he might have brought it forth himself, out of the indecipherable longings that swept him on these mornings: he felt himself melt, crumble within like winter-rotten earthworks before new rivulets. Sometimes he didn't know whether to laugh or cry.

Down on the floor of the old Rotunda as the King and his retinue went through, the patient Grays were still at their cleaning work. They had accomplished much since Sennred had first noticed them, that day Red Senlin had come to the City to be King. The tortured circle dance of kings he had seen them uncover then had proved to be not a circle but part of a spiral, part of a

History they thought, emanating from a beginning in the center to an end—where?

You must learn to pretend, dead Redhand had said when they stood here together, *if you would live here long.* Well, he was learning: would learn so well, would live here so long that he could perhaps begin to lead that spiral out of its terrible dance, lead it . . . where?

In the center of the floor, the Grays had begun to uncover bizarre images—a thing with vast sails; stars, or suns; creatures of the Deep.

Didn't the Woman in Red talk too of suns, and sails, and the Deep? She had for sure talked of bringing her news to the King. Did he dare stop, on his way Outward, to speak to her, listen to her? They had all advised him against it. A spring madness, they said, people in motion.

He stepped carefully past the grinning kings to the door Defensible, newly widened that winter. His laughing servant held a brand-new traveling cloak for him.

And what if it was not madness at all, not ephemeral? What if Time had indeed burst out of his old accustomed round, gone adventuring on some new path? Would he know? And would it matter if he did?

He took the cloak from his servant. He would see Caredd soon, and that did matter, very much.

·ABOUT THE AUTHOR

JOHN CROWLEY came to New York City from the Mid-
west in 1964, and earned his living there in films and
television. In 1977 he moved to Massachusetts, where
he has lived since in one small town or another, writing
novels.

THE WORLD FANTASY AWARD-WINNING NOVEL

"AMBITIOUS, DAZZLING, STRANGELY MOVING, A MARVELOUS MAGIC-REALIST FAMILY CHRONICLE."
—*Book World (The Washington Post)*

Little, Big
by *John Crowley*

Somewhere beyond the city, at the edge of a wildwood, sits a house on the border between reality and fantasy, a place where the lives of faeries and mortals intertwine. Sometime in our age, a young man in love comes here to be wed, and enters a family whose Tale reaches backward and forward a hundred years, from the sunlit hours of a gentler time, to the last, dark days of this century—and beyond to a new dawn.

Sensual, exuberant, witty, and wise, LITTLE, BIG is a true masterpiece, a tale of wonder you will take to your heart and treasure for years to come. It is on sale September 15, 1983, wherever Bantam paperbacks are sold, or you can use this handy coupon for ordering:

FANTASY AND SCIENCE FICTION FAVORITES

Bantam brings you the recognized classics as well as the current favorites in fantasy and science fiction. Here you will find the most recent titles by the most respected authors in the genre.

☐	23944	THE DEEP John Crowley	$2.9
☐	23853	THE SHATTERED STARS Richard McEnroe	$2.9
☐	23795	DAMIANO R. A. MacAvoy	$2.9
☐	23205	TEA WITH THE BLACK DRAGON R. A. MacAvoy	$2.7
☐	23365	THE SHUTTLE PEOPLE George Bishop	$2.9
☐	22939	THE UNICORN CREED Elizabeth Scarborough	$3.5
☐	23120	THE MACHINERIES OF JOY Ray Bradbury	$2.7
☐	22666	THE GREY MANE OF MORNING Joy Chant	$3.5
☐	23494	MASKS OF TIME Robert Silverberg	$2.9
☐	23057	THE BOOK OF SKULLS Robert Silverberg	$2.9
☐	23063	LORD VALENTINE'S CASTLE Robert Silverberg	$3.5
☐	20870	JEM Frederik Pohl	$2.9
☐	23460	DRAGONSONG Anne McCaffrey	$2.9
☐	20592	TIME STORM Gordon R. Dickson	$2.9
☐	23036	BEASTS John Crowley	$2.9
☐	23666	EARTHCHILD Sharon Webb	$2.9

Prices and availability subject to change without notice.

Buy them at your local bookstore or use this handy coupon for ordering

---

Bantam Books, Inc., Dept. SF2, 414 East Golf Road, Des Plaines, Ill. 60016

Please send me the books I have checked above. I am enclosing $_____
(please add $1.25 to cover postage and handling). Send check or money order
—no cash or C.O.D.'s please.

Mr/Mrs/Miss _____

Address_____

City_____ State/Zip_____

SF2—1/84

Please allow four to six weeks for delivery. This offer expires 7/84.